Charles Reade

Kate Peyton

Jealousy

Charles Reade

Kate Peyton
Jealousy

ISBN/EAN: 9783337342340

Printed in Europe, USA, Canada, Australia, Japan

Cover: Foto ©Andreas Hilbeck / pixelio.de

More available books at **www.hansebooks.com**

KATE PEYTON;

OR

JEALOUSY.

𝔄 𝔇𝔯𝔞𝔪𝔞

IN

A PROLOGUE AND FOUR ACTS.

BY

CHARLES READE, ESQ.

LONDON:

WILLIAMS AND STRAHAN, PRINTERS, 74 NEW CUT, LAMBETH.

1872.

Dramatis Personæ.

GRIFFITH GAUNT, ESQ. ..
GEORGE NEVILLE, ESQ. ..
MR. HAMMERSLY .. .. *(Country Gentlemen)* ..
MAJOR RICKARDS .. ..
MR. HOUSEMAN .. *(A Jovial Solicitor)* .. ..
AMOS TRIST .. *(His Doleful Clerk)* .. .. ..
FATHER FRANCIS *(An Elderly Priest)* .. .. ..
FATHER LEONARD *(A Young Priest)* .. .. ..
TOM LEICESTER .. ..
MR. HITCHIN .. .. *(A Surgeon)* .. .. ..
PAUL CARRICK .. *(A Lancashire Farrier)* .. .. ..
SERJEANT WILTSHIRE *(Counsel for the Crown)* .. ..
JUDGE .. ..
CRIER OF THE COURT .. ..
JAILOR .. ..
COURIER .. ..
BARRISTERS, CLERK OF ARRAIGNS, JAILORS,
RUSTICS, ETC.

KATE PEYTON *(Afterwards* MRS. GAUNT) .. ..
ROSE GAUNT .. *(Her Daughter)* .. .. ..
MERCY VINT .. ..
CAROLINE RYDER .. .. *(A Lady's Maid)* .. .. ..
JANE BANNISTER .. *(A Domestic Servant)* .. .. ..

DATE OF THE PROLOGUE, 1740.

A Lapse of Eight Years intervenes between the Prologue and the First Act of the Play.

PROLOGUE.

SCENE I.—*Mr. Houseman's Inner Office, communicating
with the outer office by an open door, and also by a window, which is practicable, and just large enough for* AMOS
TRIST *to put his head through.* '*In flat, door,* C, *and a
window looking on the street. A screen. Two chairs,
and a long table,* R.H., *covered with a number of briefs
and other papers. Deed boxes against the wall.*

MUSIC, *Poacher's Song.*

AMOS TRIST *discovered in the outer office at the window,
perched on a high stool, and employed engrossing a deed
on a high desk.* TOM LEICESTER *seated on the edge of*
MR. HOUSEMAN'S *table, swinging his legs* (*dress a tight suit
of grey cloth*). TOM LEICESTER *looks furtively round, whips
a piece of smooth brass wire out of his pocket, and pro-
ceeds to make a slip-noose with it, and to twist that part
of the wire double which forms the noose, leaving the rest
single. All this time his eyes are roving, and watching*
AMOS *in a manner half wild, half sly.*

TRIST. (*putting his head through the pane.*)   Tom
Leicester, what are you doing?

TOM.   Plaiting straw for my granny's bonnet.   (*Whistles
a verse of the Poacher's Song, accompanied very softly by the
orchestra.*)

TRIST. (*dolefully*).   I like that tune: it is so merry.
What tune is it?

TOM.   The old hundredth.   New style; as the gipsies
sing it in the wood, when the hares are afoot by moonlight.

TRIST.   Mr. Leicester.   Now you are promoted to be
a lawyer's clerk, please forget your gipsies and woods, and
moonshine, and take to copying—like a man.

TOM.   Forget the woods and the moonlight!   You'd

never forget them if you had ever seen them together. Do you know a dog they call a lurcher?

TRIST. I have not that honour.

TOM. Then he is half greyhound and half sheep-dog; the cleverest dog after game that goes on four feet. (*Pause.*) Well—I'm a lurcher. (*Gets down.*) For my sire was a gentleman, and my dam is a gipsy. Greyhound and sheep-dog—gentleman and gipsy, that is a cross you'll never breed a lawyer from. (*Jumps up on table, whistles as before, and dangles his feet.*)

TRIST. Your father a gentleman! Nay, but what sort of gentleman? For now-a-days every Jack is a gentleman.

TOM. A Squire, then,—a magistrate,—one of the quorum, that do a send a poor chap to gaol for wiring a hare—when they can catch him.

TRIST. Here's news. Prithee, what is his worship's name?

TOM. His name! 'Tis writ upon my forehead.

(*Exit into outer office.*)

TRIST. I now take a note of the conversation. (*Writes.*) The ju-ni-or clerk in this long-established office is a—lurcher. Whose—worshipful father's name is writ upon his forehead. (*Pause*). Then it is inscribed on brass.

(*The jovial voice of* MR. HOUSEMAN *is heard, saying—*

" Good day, Tom; good day, Amos."

(MR. HOUSEMAN *bustles in, takes off his cloak and comforter. Then sits down and rapidly sorts his papers, speaking at the same time.*)

HOUSE. My letters, Thomas, if you please. (*As* TOM *is bringing them.*) A beautiful day, lads. (*Rubs his hands.*)

TRIST. (*Lugubriously.*) I think we shall have some more snow.

HOUSE. Not a flake, sir; not a flake. My agenda!

Oh, (*takes up a paper of memoranda*) just copy these
exhibits in re Pettyfer.

(*Exit* Tom *with the exhibits.*)

(*He consults his agenda again, and turns to* Trist.)

That Will?—Mr. Neville's. Have you got it engrossed?
You know, he said he must sign it to-day, to-morrow
might be too late. What on earth did he mean by that?

Trist (*who has resumed his work*). Ay; what indeed?
I don't like the looks of it.

House. Ha! ha! Did you ever like the looks of
anything in the world, you croaking young raven? (*While
speaking, opens all his letters, and spreads them out flat
before he reads one.*)

Trist. (*bringing in will.*) Here's Mr. Neville's will,
sir, duly engrossed.

(Houseman *takes will, and runs his eye rapidly over it.*)

Trist. (*Rebelliously.*) Well, I daresay I do croak a
bit. But why is this young gentleman in such haste to
make his will? and why (*pointing to a clause in will*) does
he leave Moulton Grange to (*the lawyer and clerk put their
heads together over the clause*) the—very—lady that young
Griffith Gaunt has wooed this four years? These Gaunts
are dangerous. They are known for four things. First,
for jealousy; secondly, for fighting on their legs till they
can't stand; thirdly, for fighting on their backs till they
can't breathe; fourthly, for long, black moles on their—
foreheads—Oh! (*aside*) the lurcher there has got a
mole – written—on his forehead.

House. Why, here's a letter from the lady herself.
Fine as a hair. (*Puts on his spectacles and reads*)—
" Dear Mr. Houseman,

        " If the hounds kill within ten miles of your office,
" expect a visit from me. Prithee be not from home.
                " Your loving friend,
                        " And humble servant,
                                " Kate Peyton.

" *Postscriptum.*—Dear—good—kind Mr. Houseman, I
" have been so imprudent." (*He leans back in his chair.*)

(A TIMID KNOCK IS HEARD.)

TRIST. There, sir, there. She has been so imprudent. Now, put this (*taps letter*) and that (*taps deed*) together; and I say mischief is a brewing. And, as usual, there's a woman

MUSIC.

(*Enter quickly* KATE PEYTON, *in a scarlet riding habit and purple jockey cap, doeskin gauntlets, boots, and one spur, light hunting whip, with gold hook, &c., followed by* TOM LEICESTER, *who stands delighted in the doorway.*

at the bottom of it. Oh !

(KATE PEYTON *curtsies low to* HOUSEMAN *and* TRIST, *who bow low.*)

KATE. Good day, gentlemen. (*Pause.*) Do I interrupt you ?

HOUSE. Nay, madam. Beauty takes precedence of business; be seated. (*They seat her.*) Never heed Amos Trist; he is as close as the grave, and almost as cheerful. Haw! haw! Heyday, what are *you* standing there for, with eyes like saucers ?

TOM. Why, to hear all about the hunt, to be sure. (*Pathetically.*) Oh, please do, mistress. Oh Lord, at the sight of you and your little blue bonnet, that I've seen a leading the field so often, I'm all afire.

HOUSE. (*starting up.*) You incurable young vagabond; think you this lady comes hither to chat with the likes of you ?

KATE (*quietly.*) Nay, good Mr. Houseman, do not scold the young gentleman. He seems an enthusiast. But indeed, young sir, though I ride hard to hounds in my excitement, I love not to describe that folly in cold blood. And to-day I have something very serious to confide to my old friend here.

HOUSE. (*Sotto voce to the clerks.*) The lady would be private.   (*Exeunt* TOM *and* AMOS.) Now, madam.

KATE. You know, Mr. Houseman, I look on you as a father. So I—I—I wish you were a woman.

HOUSE. Nay, madam; there is no *sex* in a lawyer's office. My female clients come here and tell me things they dare not tell their grandmothers.

KATE (*brightening up.*) Oh, do they? Then so will I. It is about two gentlemen.

HOUSE. Well, that is only one too many.

KATE. I beg your pardon; it is two too many for me. Well then, sir, you know Mr. Gaunt has followed me this four years, and, I believe, loves me sincerely. But I am a Catholic; he is a Protestant. And Mr. George Neville has come back from Italy, and he pays me great attention; and the other day his famous piebald was standing in our yard, and I was so incautious as to jump on him and give him a gallop; out comes Mr. Neville, who has always his wits about him, and carries off my old grey in exchange. Both horses are well known in the county, and the matter spread like wildfire. Six noodles toasted me and Mr. Neville together, six boobies rang the church bells, and, Mr. Houseman, I am compromised.

HOUSE. Well, to be frank, I think you are. Hnmph! Let me see. You have no decided preference for either of these gentlemen?

KATE. No.

HOUSE. You are not—in love—with either?

KATE. (*Scornfully.*) In love? Goodness forbid!

HOUSE. Then your course is clear. Mr. Neville has large estates of his own; he is heir to a baronetcy: you admire him; he loves you: 'tis with him you are compromised. You must marry him.

(*Pause.*)

KATE. Yes. But then—what is to become of Mr. Gaunt?

HOUSE. He must go to sea, like his father before him.

KATE. ·Yes, to be sure. (*Pause.*) The worst of it is, he loves me so. He has been my servant this four years.

Poor soul, he has often rid fifteen miles and back for a
word with me at our shrubbery gate. I should break his
heart. Mr. Neville? Why, he is a gay, good-humoured
rake, who only plays at love. He has too much vanity;
too much spirit, and too much sense to sigh long for
any woman. I am only his pastime.

HOUSE. Madam, you are mistaken. Mr. Neville has a
deep and sincere affection for you.

KATE. How can you know that?

HOUSE. Got the proof in this office. On *parchment.*

KATE. Then show it me. Seeing is believing.

HOUSE. Nay, I demur to that. It is not our custom
to betray the secrets of our clients.

A KNOCK AT THE OUTER OFFICE.

TRIST. (*From his seat.*) That is Mr. Neville. Shall I
show him in?

KATE. Not whilst I am here; oh pray. Or let me get
into covert first. (*Goes to screen.*) May I? I won't
listen—if I can help it. (*Conceals herself.*)

HOUSE. (*Going towards door.*) Of course you won't.
That is off my conscience. Be good enough to come in,
sir.

Enter GEORGE NEVILLE.

We are quite ready for you. Be seated. (*They sit.*) I'll
just read the will over before we sign. There's the draft
to compare.

(*He hands* MR. NEVILLE *the draft, who sprinkles it with a
scent bottle, but never looks at it to read it.* HOUSEMAN
then reads very fast.)

  " I, George Neville, of Neville's Court, in the county
" of Cumberland, and of Leicester Square, London, Esq.,
" being this day of sound mind, memory and understanding,
" do deliver this as my last will and testament. First, I
" bequeath my body,"—etc.,—"and my soul,"—the
usual form. "I desire my executors to discharge my
" funeral and testamentary expenses—"

(MR. NEVILLE, *early in this tirade, puts his fingers in his (ears, and shows signs of distress.*)

NEV. Hold, sir! Would you assassinate me with verbiage? I came here to sign a will.

HOUSE. What, without reading it?

NEV. Of course. I'll *sign* any rigmarole you like, but I wouldn't listen to it for a great deal of money. (HOUSE. *looks amazed.*) Stay; there's a passage in the thing which ought to be interesting, for it contains the name of a lady for whom I have a profound esteem. You shall read me that part, if you don't mind the trouble.

HOUSE. I will, sir, with great pleasure. Ahem! (*Reads loudly and distinctly.*) "And I give and bequeath " to Mistress Catherine Peyton, of Peyton Hall, in the " said county, in token of my respect and regard, all that " my freehold estate, called Moulton Grange, with the " messuage or tenement standing and being thereon, and " the farmyard, buildings and appurtenances belonging " thereto, and which contains, by estimation, 376 acres " 3 roods and 5 perches, to hold to her, the said Catherine " Peyton, her heirs and assigns—for ever."

NEV. There—hang the rest. Now let me sign, and bid you good day.

(*Enter* AMOS TRIST.)

(*Business of signing, sealing and delivering.*)

(*They rise*)

HOUSE. Ah, sir, few young gentlemen of your age have the prudence to make their wills. They confound youth with immortality.

NEV. (*offers him snuff.*) Not when they know it is an even chance whether they live the day out or not.

(*Exit, with a polite bow, leaving* HOUSEMAN *with the pinch suspended.* KATE *comes out, looking very thoughtful and subdued.* MR. H. *turns and sees her near him.*)

HOUSE. Well, madam, what think you of all this?

KATE. Oh, sir, I am surprised; I am flattered. Poor

A 2

Mr. Neville! Heaven forbid I should ever inherit his
Moulton Grange. (*Walks restlessly.*) I am uneasy. This
gentleman is in the flower of his youth. Why does he
make his will; and in such haste? (*Pause.*) Pray, what
did he say to you at the door? for I only caught one word.

TRIST. (*Pokes his head through window, and whispers*)
Are you at home?

HOUSE. How can *I* tell? Till I know my visitor.

TRIST. Mr. Griffith Gaunt.

KATE. There now!—Get rid of him as quickly as you
can; that we may resume our conversation.

(*Retires behind screen.*)

HOUSE. Show him in.

MUSIC, *short and grave.*

(*Enter* GRIFFITH GAUNT, *sombre and depressed as a man
who thinks he has not long to live.*)

GAUNT. Mr. Houseman—I am come to make my will.

(HOUSEMAN *stares.—A pause.*)

HOUSE. Why, the world is turning wise. You are
right, sir: the young are as mortal as the old, and if any
creature on earth deserves to be hanged, it is—the man
who dies intestate.

GAUNT. Then here is my will. Be pleased to witness
it for me. (*Produces a scrap of paper written on.*)

HOUSE. That thing a will! Why, it would all go into
the ace of spades.

GAUNT. I had not time to waste words. Shall I read
it to you? (HOUSEMAN *nods stiffly.* GAUNT *reads.*) "I
" Griffith Gaunt, at present residing at Bolton Hall, in
" the county of Cumberland, do deliver this as my
" last will and testament. I bequeath all the property,
" real or personal, which I now possess, or may hereafter
" become entitled to, to my dear friend and mistress,
" Catherine Peyton, of Peyton Hall. But I also bequeath
" my curse to the said Catherine Peyton, if at any time

" she shall wed with George Neville, of Neville's Court,
" in this county."

HOUSE. I object to the last clause. You cannot
demise a curse: it is neither realty nor personalty.
Besides, sir, when a Christian man makes his last will
and testament, he should think of the grave, and of the
place beyond, where we may carry our love for those we
leave behind, but not our hate nor our jealousy: the gate
is too narrow for such wares.

GAUNT (*doggedly*). Old man, be not too hard on me:
I am no saint nor apostle, but a poor, plain gentleman of
Cumberland: happy as a prince two little months ago;
but now a stranger has come between me and her I love.
My whole bleeding heart lies on this paper. I can't cut it in
two and take half back. But I'll tell you what I can do, I can
carry it to that new lawyer over the way, if Jack Houseman has forgotten who set him up in this town, and backed
him against high and low, when I was in my cradle.

HOUSE. (*agitated.*) Here, Amos; come in directly,
and witness this damnable instrument with me.

(*Re-enter* TRIST.)

(*Business of signing and delivering the will, as the testator's
act and deed.*)

HOUSE. There, sir, you see I have not forgotten old
Squire Gaunt, my benefactor. What more can I do for
his son?

GAUNT. (*Giving him his hand.*) Nothing. You have
set my heart at ease. Oh, yes, by-the-bye, let me have
a word in private with young Tom Leicester.

HOUSE. Certainly. I'll look over his work in the
outer office. Here, Tom Leicester, come and speak to
Squire Gaunt. (*Exeunt* HOUSEMAN *and* TRIST.)

(*Re-enter* TOM LEICESTER.)

GAUNT. Tom, come here. Look at me, lad. Canst
keep a secret?

TOM. Ay, Squire, that I can.

GAUNT. (*Lowering his voice.*)   I'm going from this place to Scutchemzee Nob—to fight Mr. Neville.

(KATE *shows her face for an instant, and is evidently trying to listen.*)

Come after me by the footpath, as fast as you can; and if I fall, take this letter to Peyton Hall on the instant. If I stand, give it back to me.

TOM.   Only let me get my own things on, Squire, and I'll do your bidding. I can't run in these.

GAUNT.   Well, well; but lose no time. (TOM *runs out.* (*Looks at his watch.*)   I must ride hard too; 'tis near the hour.   *Exit.*

(KATE *comes forward, pale and agitated.*)

KATE.   What mystery is this ?

(*Re-enter* MR. HOUSEMAN.)

Mr. Houseman !   Both these gentlemen's lives are in danger: that is why they make their wills. And how should both their lives be in danger, but from each other ? But perhaps the letter will tell me.

(TOM *runs in in his gipsy clothes.*)

Ah ! I know you now. The brave boy that runs with he hounds. The letter, the letter ! I know it is for me,

TOM.   Nay, but I wa'n't to give you that. Not till I see which of them gets killed.

KATE.   Which gets killed !   (*To* HOUSEMAN.)   There— there !   (*Holds out her hands imploringly.*)   Oh ! for pity's sake do not keep it from me !

TOM.   There, then.   (*Gives her letter.*)

KATE (*Reading it.*)   " Sweet mistress,—When this " reaches you, I shall be no more here to trouble you with " my jealousy. This Neville set it abroad that you had " changed horses with him. He is a liar, and I told him " so to his teeth. (Oh, madman ! he has insulted the bravest gentleman in the county !)   " We are to meet at " three this afternoon, and one must die."   (*She puts her hand on her head, and is transfixed with horror.*)   One

must die! "Then let the grave hide my faults from thy
" memory; think only that I loved thee well. I leave thee
" my substance—would it were ten times more—and the
" last thought of my heart.   .

> " So, no more in this world, from him that
> " is thy true lover and humble servant,
> " till death,

" GRIFFITH GAUNT."

·(*Crying convulsively*) What have I done? What shall I
do? Oh, Mr. Houseman, pray stop this fearful fighting.
Pray! pray! pray! (*Clings sobbing to him.*)

HOUSE. Alas, my dear! what can I do? I don't
even know where the duel is to be.

TOM. But I do. (*Pulls Kate's sleeve, and whimpers*)
Mistress, don't ye take on like that. While there's life
there's hope. I'll show you a short cut to Scutchemzee
Nob, where the fighting is to be. (KATE *starts up*) But
nay, I forgot; there's Harrowden Brook in the way, and
it is running broad and deep, with the flood. (*Shakes his
head.*)

KATE. Harrowden Brook! I took it flying twice to-
day, after a miserable fox, and shall I shy it when there's
life to be saved? Oh, you brave boy, run to the inn,—
you will go faster on foot than I can; bring out my piebald
this moment, and then just put me in the line for Scutchemzee Nob, that is all. Fly! fly! (TOM *runs out.*)

HOUSE. But, madam, had you not better trust to a
constable's warrant? To go on the field will compromise
you worse than ever.

KATE. What does that matter, in a case of life and
death? Sir, I have acted like a coquette and a vacillating
fool; but God, he knows, I'm neither. I have the best
horse in all the north country, and I've the heart to ride him;
and I *will* ride him on to their drawn swords, sooner than
any man's blood shall be shed for me. (*Exit running.*)

HOUSE. (*Shouting.*) She is on fire, and I've caught the
flame! Here, Amos! Turn out, ye dog. Shall we be

outdone by a woman ? Come ! give me my alderman's staff
—quick !—I'll tap them on the shoulder, and stop their
fighting. Shut you the office, and away we go to Scutchemzee Nob.

A HORN IS BLOWN.

What's that ?

COURIER. (*outside.*) Express from London, for John
Houseman, Attorney-at-law.

HOUSE. I'm coming down this moment. I'm coming.
(*Exit hastily.*)

SCENE II.—*Outside* HOUSEMAN'S *door, on which his name
appears on a plate.*

MUSIC.

Enter a COURIER *in jack boots, splashed.* HOUSEMAN *comes
out, followed by* TRIST.

HOUSE. Come, my lad, despatch. For I'm in a
hurry.

COURIER. Despatch ! Why, I've knocked up two
horses between this and Lancaster. Isn't that despatch ?
From Atkins and Co., Attorneys, Gray's Inn, London.

*Hands him a packet, consisting of a letter and the draft of
a will. He hands the document to* TRIST, *who runs his
eye over it, while* HOUSEMAN *reads the letter.*)

HOUSE. (*Reads.*) " Dear Sir,—This is to inform you
" that your client, Mr. Charlton, has just breathed his
" last, after an illness of two days only. Finding himself
" near his end, he sent for our Mr. Atkins, and made his
" will, revoking all previous dispositions of his property.
" In this, his last testament, his heir-at-law, though a
" Catholic, is made residuary legatee. We send you the
" draft," &c., &c. Let me see the last clause. It is so.
Hurrah ! There's a guinea to the bearer of good news.
(*Exit* COURIER, L.H.)

Well, this settles all; she marries Mr. Neville, unless،
we have got to bury him. Ah ! there goes scarlet and

blue, on her great piebald, slap through the churchyard, by heaven; and over the wall, like a bird! Come, let us get horses and a guide to the Nob; and the devil take the hindmost. *(Exit.)*

TRIST. *(Lugubriously).* Then he is sure to take me.
(Exit.)

SCENE III.—*Scutchemzee Nob. A bleak, rising ground, looking down on a long, sloping valley. The trees are covered with rime, or light frost.* GRIFFITH GAUNT *standing pale, gloomy, and dejected, in position,* L.H. MR. NEVILLE *in position,* R.C.B. MR. HITCHIN, *a Surgeon,* L.R., *with a case of surgical instruments. In the* C., *between the combatants, stand the seconds,* MR. HAMMERSLY *and* MAJOR RICKARDS—*the latter has finished loading two brace of pistols.*

MUSIC, *of a grave character, not loud.*

MAJOR RICKARDS *places two pistols behind his back a moment, then offers* HAMMERSLY *the choice.* HAMMERSLY *takes one, and bows formally, then goes with it to* NEVILLE, RICKARDS *to* GAUNT.

MUSIC CEASES, *as the seconds turn to go to the combatants.*

RICK. *(Sotto voce.)* Stand sharp; and don't take your eye off him. *(Pause.)* How d'ye feel?

GAUNT. Like a man who must die; but will try not to die alone.

(The seconds take their places.)

RICK. Gentlemen, you will fire when I let fall this handkerchief, and not before. Mark me, gentlemen, to prevent mistakes, I shall say — one — two—three—and then drop the handkerchief. *(Pause.)* Are you both ready?

NEV. and GAUNT. Yes.

RICK. *(With white handkerchief.)* One—two—three.

(He drops the handkerchief—the combatants fire, and MR.

NEVILLE'S *hat is knocked off, and* GAUNT'S *pistol falls out of his grasp, and his right arm appears powerless. They all gather round him, except* NÉVILLE, *who, however, takes a step or two towards him.*)

HITCH. He is wounded.

GAUNT. It is nothing; it is nothing. I shoot better with my left than with my right. Give me another pistol, I say. He has hit me. And now I'll hit him.

HAM. The affair need go no farther. Mr. Neville has owned to me there was some provocation on our side. And on behalf of the party insulted, I shall let the matter end here, Mr. Gaunt being wounded.

GAUNT. (*Grimly.*) I demand my second shot to his third. He will not decline, unless he is a poltroon, as well as—what I called him.

NEV. Hammersly, you are wasting time there. Load again; and let me rid the county of a mad dog.

GAUNT. Rickards, I don't insult my rival in the field. I content myself—with killing him.

MUSIC, SUBDUED.

(*Business of loading pistols, o., during which the following dialogue, sotto voce:*—)

HAM. This is a barbarous business.

RICK. It *is* business. It is not play. I think my man will wing yours this time. I see it in his eye.

HAM. Neville is a dead shot, when he chooses. I am afraid neither will live long after this discharge.

(*Seconds return to their places.*)

RICK. (*Solemnly.*) Gentlemen, we are both resolved that this is the last shot you can be allowed to fire in this quarrel, under any circumstances. Are you ready?

NEV. and GAUN. Yes.

RICK. Then—one—two—

(KATE PEYTON *rushes in and stands in the line of fire She looks from one to the other. The combatants lower their pistols, and stand aghast. Then they take off their hats,*

and NEVILLE *puts his pistol behind his back.* KATE
curtsies low to each.

KATE. (*Walking majestically up to* GAUNT.) Give me
that pistol, Mr. Gaunt.

(*He gives it her submissively. She walks to* MR. NEVILLE.)

Oblige me with yours, Mr. Neville. .

(*He bows and hands it her. She returns to centre, and,
standing with her back to audience, fires both pistols in
the air, and drops them. Then turns and lifts her eyes
and hands to Heaven in gratitude. Her lips move as if in
prayer—then she utters a faint cry, and falls in swoon,
* C. *The gentlemen utter exclamations of dismay, and rush
to her assistance.*

GAUNT. We have killed her! we have killed her!
HITCH. Stand aside, gentlemen, if you please.
GAUNT. Oh, yes, the doctor! Oh, sir!
HITCH. Be calm, gentlemen, pray be calm. (*Ex-
amining her.*) The lady has swooned, that is all.
HAM. Clap her hands!
RICK. Burnt feathers!
NEV. (*Bustling up.*) Here's my scent bottle.
GAUNT. Here's my flask!
HITCH. No, no. Fetch me some cold water.
            GAUNT *and* NEVILLE *rush out,* R. & L.)

RICK. Shall I raise her head?
HITCH. On the contrary, the flatter she lies the better.
(*Coolly.*) Swooning is caused by the blood receding from
the vessels of the brain.

(*Re-enter, running,* NEVILLE *and* GAUNT, *each with water
in his hat, which they thrust under Surgeon's nose.*)

HITCH. (*Dipping a hand into each hat, flings water
sharply into* KATE's *face*) There—she is coming to. Be
pleased to stand aloof, and give her air. And you mustn't
be alarmed if she's a little hysterical at first.

(*They stand aloof, but watch her with marked anxiety. She

*sighs and looks bewildered.   Presently she turns her head
and sees* NEVILLE *and* GAUNT.)

KATE.   Oh !   (*Hides her face in her hands*).
HITCH.   Courage, madam.   There are none here but
friends.   (KATE *begins to cry.*)   Now, Mr. Gaunt, your
flask.   There, Mistress Kate, drink a drop, to oblige old
Hitchin, that brought you into the world.   'Twill do you
good now.

(KATE *clings to* HITCHIN, *and sips from flask, crying a little
all the while.*)

KATE.   (*Recovering a little.*)   This comes of my fasting
so long.   I have eaten nothing since breakfast.   It is
enough to upset anybody.
GAUN.   (*Coaxing*).   Yes, and 'you had a hard run with
the hounds, too.
NEV.   (*Coaxing.*)   It was enough to upset a porter.
KATE.   (*Rising.*)   But indeed I did not come here to make
a fuss, but to clear up a misunderstanding.   Gentlemen,
thus it is.   I took the freedom to borrow Mr. Neville's
piebald horse.
GAUNT.   Oh, if you did exchange horses with him, of
course I have only to make my apologies—and go.
KATE.   Be pleased not to exaggerate, sir, where I am
concerned.   The exchange, as you call it, was only for a
day.   But Mr. Neville knows his piebald is worth two of
my grey; and so he was too fine a gentleman to send me
back my old hunter, and demand his young thoroughbred.
He waited for me to do that; and if anybody ought to be
shot, it is me.   But, as I am not so fond of being shot
as some people are—here, Mr. Leicester !

(*Enter* TOM LEICESTER.)

Put my side saddle on that grey horse yonder, and the
man's saddle on the piebald.   (*Exit* TOM LEICESTER.)
GAUNT.   (*With joy.*)   Ah !
KATE.   And now, Mr. Gaunt, it is your turn.   You
must apologise.

GAUNT. To him!—Never!

KATE. Come, consider: Mr. Neville is esteemed by all the county. (*Draws nearer to him.*) Oblige me, and do what is right.

GAUNT. She sides with him. Oh, agony!

KATE. Come, Griffith, let your reason unsay the barbarous words your passion has uttered against a worthy gentleman, whom we all esteem. (*Pause.*) Mr. Neville, Mr. Gaunt has a word to say to you.

(*She draws back,* NEVILLE *and* GAUNT *approach, the latter dejectedly, and salute.*)

GAUNT. (*Dejectedly, but not sulkily.*) Sir, one, whom I am little used to gainsay, has made me see that I was too hasty, and applied harsher terms to you than the occasion justified: and—so—sir—

NEV. Not a word more, sir, I pray. I do not feel quite blameless in the matter, and have no wish to mortify an honourable adversary. I am satisfied.

(*They bow, and separate.* GAUNT *leans against a tree, and beckons* HITCHIN *and* RICKARDS. *These are promptly joined . by* HAMMERSLY, *and the gentlemen conceal* GAUNT *from* KATE, *while the Doctor cuts off the sleeve of* GAUNT'S *coat, and cuts out a bullet, which operation, however, is not to be made too clear to the audience. During the first part of this business* KATE's *attention is distracted by her conversation with* MR. NEVILLE.)

KATE. That was kind and generous of you. May I go away now? You promise me there will be no more fighting?

NEV. Oh, all that is over for to-day. Do you really care about two fools like Gaunt and me shooting one another?

KATE. Strange to say, I do. If either of you had died for me, my life would have been one long remorse.

NEV. Then let me remind you that you can end the difference at once—by honouring one of us with your hand.

KATE. (*Drily.*) Which ?

NEV. The one you think you can love.

HITCH. It is close to the skin.

(KATE *turns her eyes with curiosity on the other group.*)

GAUNT. Cut away, man. If you cut my arm off, I should not feel it. Here lies my wound. (*Lays his hand on his breast.*)

KATE. (*Uneasily.*) What are they all so busy about round Mr. Gaunt ?

NEV. (*Coolly.*) I have not an idea.

HITCH. Out it comes, I've got it. Now put on this sling.

KATE. (*Advancing.*) What is the matter ! Wounded ! —He is wounded !

RICK. A mere trifle, madam; no danger. See, here is the bullet.

KATE. Ah ! ah ! (*Looks askant and horror-stricken at bullet.*) Give me that bullet; it is mine. He owes it to me. Ha ! ha ! ha ! (*Laughs hysterically.*)

(*Surgeon puts on sling*)

HOUSEMAN. (*Outside.*) Hurrah ! hurrah !

MUSIC.

(*Enter* HOUSEMAN, *hastily, followed by* AMOS TRIST.)

HOUSE. Good news ! Hurrah ! Thank Heaven you are all alive to hear it, especially you, Mr. Neville. Madam, I wish you joy.

KATE. (*Angrily.*) Oh, don't come wishing *me* joy; wish me a halter. (*Eyes the bullet.*) For that is what I deserve.

HOUSE. Mr. Charlton is dead, and you are his residuary legatee

KATE. (*Impatiently.*) Residuary legatee ! What is that ?

HOUSE. Why, he has revoked his old will, and left Mr. Gaunt two thousand pounds: but to you he leaves (*reading from will*) all his messuages or tenements, farm lands, hereditaments and real estate, &c. &c.

TRIST. And all his moneys, mortgages, chattels, furniture, plate, pictures, wines, liquors, horses.

HOUSE. In a word, all he had in the world, to you, and your heirs, executors, administrators, and assigns for ever. Madam, I wish you joy.

TRIST. (*Dolefully.*) Madam, I wish you joy.

KATE. What, I have wounded him, and disinherited him, and you wish me joy? Monsters of cruelty!

HOUSE. Heyday!

GAUNT. Nay, Kate, look not at it so. (*In a broken voice.*) Gentlemen, never did good fortune light on one more worthy. And, for me, I feel not the loss of house and lands, not one jot. I have lost this day what I valued a thousand times more than them. Your arm, Rickards. (*Leans on him.*)

KATE. (*To* NEVILLE.) You are right; and I can hide my heart no more. Be generous; understand me, forgive me; and leave me.

NEV. (*With a magnanimous effort.*) I know how to respect a lady's will, madam.

(*He bows low—she curtsies—and exit* NEVILLE.)

KATE. (*Agitated, and lowering her eyes.*) Gentlemen, I desire to say a word in private to Mr. Gaunt.

RICK. By all means. (*They retire back, but watch.*)

KATE. (*With great emotion.*) Dear Griffith, I never loved but you. I feared your jealousy, and the difference in our faith, that is all. But this day you are wounded for my sake, and disinherited for my sake, and—oh! it is more than I can bear! My hand and my heart are yours for ever, if you will take them. Oh, Griffith! my poor, poor Griffith!

GAUNT. (*Falling on his knees, and kissing her hand passionately*). Kate! darling Kate!

KATE. Dearest, compose yourself, and don't make me cry so. Gentlemen, he is only asking my pardon.

TRIST. He is jealous; she is high-minded: she is a Catholic; he is a Protestant: I don't much like the looks——

(HOUSEMAN *stops his mouth.*)

KATE. Get up, dear, and invite the gentlemen for this day month.

GAUNT. A whole month!

KATE. I meant this day week.

MUSIC TO END.

GAUNT. This day week we hope you will do us the honour to be at our wedding.

(KATE *and* GAUNT *make a low obeisance to the others, back to the Audience: then turn and repeat the same to front.*

END OF PROLOGUE.

EIGHT YEARS ELAPSE BETWEEN THIS AND FIRST ACT.

ACT I.

Scene I.—*The Grounds of Ernshaw Castle. In front, a gravel path, bordered with box. Then a piece of turf at the side of the mere or lake. One or more flowering bushes overhang the water, and are reflected in it. On the turf, near the water, are laid one or two wet cloths and towels. A stone roller at side.*

Music.

Caroline Ryder *and* Jane Bannister *discovered.* Ryder, *dressed almost like a lady, is knitting a silk purse mechanically, but bending her brows and deep in thought. Jane is in working attire, and bare armed, and is seated on a low three-legged stool, with her coarse apron to her eyes, crying quietly; by her side is a large red pan, containing wet linen, and a basin.* Ryder *gives her a glance of perfect indifference, and pursues her reflections.*

Music changes.

(Jane *rises up with a movement of sudden resolution, takes a wet cloth out of pan, wrings it vigorously and makes it flap, then lays it on the grass behind* Ryder.)

Music ceases.

Ryder. Am I really so mad as to love him? What can come of it but misery?

(Jane, *who has returned to the stool, takes out another cloth and wrings it, but breaks down suddenly, and puts it to her eyes.*)

Jane. To be turned off like this all at one time! What will father say? He won't believe but what 'tis all my fault. He'll give me a hiding. Turn your back, if you please; I be a going to drown myself in this here mere. (*Runs towards it—Ryder takes no notice whatever.*) Ah! Ah!

Ryder. (*Without moving.*) What now?

Jane. I seed one of them nasty great fish, awaiting to

eat me up. (*Shakes her fist at the water.*) I won't die there. They'd clean the flesh off my bones in about an hour, as they did off t' parson's as was drowned there sixty years agone. (*Returns to stool, sits down and rocks.*) But I'll find some way. I won't go home, I won't never go home. Oh! oh! oh! (*Rocking.*)

RYDER. (*Tapping her on the shoulder.*) Come, Jane, don't be a fool.

JANE. (*Sobbing.*) I will. I will.

RYDER. Ah! (*Her face is wreathed in smiles.*)

MUSIC.

Enter GRIFFITH GAUNT, *with a face very ruddy and bright.*

GAUNT. Hey-day, lasses, what is your trouble?

JANE. (*Sobbing.*) I've got the sack; that is what ails me.

GAUNT. (*Rather kindly.*) Got the sack, Jenny! Why, what for?

JANE. Nay, sir, that is what I want to know. Our Dame ne'er found a fault in me; and now she does pack me off like a dog.

RYDER. Come, you must not blame the mistress. She is a good mistress as ever breathed. I'll tell you the truth, master, if you will pass me your word I shan't be sent away for it.

GAUNT. I pledge you my word as a gentleman.

RYDER. Well, then, sir, Jane's fault is yours and mine. She is not a Papist. I listened, and heard the Priest Leonard tell our Dame she must have Catholic servants. That Leonard's word is law in this house; so Harriet she was packed off last month, and now poor Jane is to go—for walking to church behind you, sir. But there, Jane, I believe he would get our very master out of the house if he could; and then what would become of us all? (*The women interchange a furtive glance.*)

GAUNT. That is enough, Jenny, thou'lt stay.

(*Exit, looking discomposed.*)

JANE. (*Who has risen.*) Mrs. Ryder, I never thought to like you so well. (*Gives her a hearty kiss, which* RYDER *receives like a martyr.*) I won't cry no more. After all (*Business,*) this house is no place for us that be women. A fine roost to be sure, where the hen she crows, and the cock do but cluck.

RYDER.   You foolish woman, there are dogs that bark, and dogs that bite. Our master is one of those that bite. Whist! here she comes, reading that book Leonard gave her. He wrote it.

Enter MRS. GAUNT, *walking very slowly, and in profound contemplation—the women curtsey, which she acknowledges, but almost without taking her eyes off the book. She stops.*

KATE.   What tenderness! what pious eloquence! How his words lift the soul above the vanities, the follies, and even the affections of this sorry world.

(*Enter* GAUNT, *hastily, meeting her.*)

Ah! my dear.

GAUNT.   I want to speak to you.

KATE. (*Closing the book and putting it in her bosom.*) With all my heart.

GAUNT.   Run away, you girls.   D'ye hear?

(RYDER *and* JANE *go out different ways, exchanging a rapid look of intelligence.*)

So Jane is turned off now.

· KATE. (*Calmly.*) I don't know about being turned off; but she leaves me next month, and Cicely Davis comes back.

GAUNT.   Cicely Davis!   An useless slut that cannot boil a potatoe fit to eat. But then she is a Papist, and poor Jenny is a Protestant, and can cook a dinner.

KATE.   My dear, do not you trouble about the women servants; leave them to me.

· GAUNT.   And welcome'; but this is not your doing, it is that Leonard's. Come, Kate, now I ask you, is a young bachelor a fit person to govern a man's family?

KATE.   A young bachelor! whoever heard of such a term applied to a priest : and a saint upon earth ?

GAUNT.   Why, he is not married, so he must be a

B

bachelor; and I say again it is monstrous for a young
bachelor to come between old married folk, and hear all
their secrets, and set up to be master of my house, and
order *my wife* to turn away *my servants*, for going to church
behind me. Why not turn *me* away too? Their fault is mine.

KATE. Griffith, you are in a passion, and I think you
want to put me in one.

GAUNT. Well, perhaps I am. But you were never so
uncharitable, nor so unreasonable, when good old Father
Francis was your director. 'Tis this Leonard's doing. He
is my secret, underhand enemy; I feel him undermining
me, inch by inch, and I can bear it no longer. I must
make a stand somewhere, and I may as well make it here;
for Jenny is a good girl, and her folk live in the village, and
she helps them. Think better of it, Kate, and let the poor
wench stay, though she does go to church behind your
husband.

KATE. Are you going to be jealous again? jealous of
my confessor? or *(fixing her eyes on him)* is some mischief-
making woman advising *you*? You never used to interfere
between me and my maids.

GAUNT. Nor wouldn't now. But this has been traced
home to the priest, and I'll not brook it. I tell you plainly,
if you turn this poor lass off, to please this mischief-
making, meddling priest, I'll turn the priest off, to please
her and her folk. They are as good as he is anyway.

KATE. As good as he is!—Now I *see* some vulgar
woman's tongue has been at your ear. The scum of my
kitchen as good as Father Leonard! you will make me
hate the mischief-making hussy. She shall pack out of
this house to-morrow morning.

GAUNT. Then I say that priest shall never darken my
doors again.

KATE. Ah! Then I say they are my doors; not yours:
and that holy man shall brighten them whenever he pleases.

GAUNT. Oh!

(Dead silence as long as possible.)

KATE. *(Aside in a whisper.)*   Oh God! what have I said?

. Music.

(*Enter* Father Francis.)

Fran. Good day, my good friends. What, are you in trouble? Perchance I intrude.

Gaunt. No, no; an old friend is always welcome—to me, at all events.

Kate. Never so welcome as now. Father, I have just committed a great sin. Ah! they may well say anger is a short madness. Was it really Kate Gaunt who said that—to Griffith?

Fran. Said what?

Kate. Ask him. I could not utter in cold blood the base, ungenerous thing I have said in anger.

(Francis *looks towards* Gaunt.)

Gaunt. And I have nothing to say about this lady to any man. She is my wife. (Francis *pats him on the back approvingly.*) Ah, Father Francis, you are an honest man : why did you leave us? We were happy together all those years that she had your advice to walk by.

Fran. (*Thoughtfully*) My successor, Brother Leonard, is much my superior in piety. To be sure, I am older and more experienced.

Kate. Let me profit by both. Come with me to my boudoir. Receive my confession, inflict my penance, and aid me with your counsels.

(*Sighs, and exit, followed by* Francis.)

Gaunt. It is true. Both house and land are hers; tied up as tight as wax. *She* said "No," in her grand way; "shall I give him myself, and grudge him my lands?" But the priests had their will. Even my two thousand pounds is hers now, for I spent it on this place. Eight years man and wife, and, till this day, she has always put me forward as the Squire, and made herself of no importance ; but the moment I set up my authority against that young priest's—"Know your real place, Griffith

GAUNT. This is my house, not yours; your place in it is on a low stool, at Leonard's feet."—REVENGE!

Enter THOMAS LEICESTER, *with a bucket.*

What have you got there?

TOM. Pike—for our Papists.

GAUNT. Put 'em down, and listen to me. I hear you are sick of my service, and want to be a pedlar, only you haven't got the money to fill your pack. There's five guineas. (TOM *takes them and looks stupified.*) Now tell me; why do I that for thee?

TOM. Well, Squire, you had always an open hand, and I have been a good servant, and kept your honour's game.

GAUNT. You never catch a poacher, and you wire my rabbits, and sell them at the nearest market.

(TOM *hangs his head.*)

I ought to send thee to Carlisle Gaol on a justice's warrant; instead of that I empty my pockets into thine. Why do I so? Come, speak thy mind for once, or else begone for a liar as well as a poacher.

(TOM *looks to see that they are alone.*)

TOM. Well, sir, since we are alone, 'tis this here mole I am in debt to, no doubt.

(*Takes off his cap and shows mole.* GRIFFITH *shows his.* RYDER *re-enters at back, and affects to busy herself with the linen.*)

GAUNT. Tom, I've been insulted.

TOM. That won't pass. Who is the man?

GAUNT. One I cannot call out like a gentleman, and must not lay on with my cane. But you might deal with him. 'Tis the Popish priest, Father Leonard.

TOM. Say ye so, Squire? Then a word in your ear. First time he comes here, George and I will take him by the heels and drag him through the horsepond. A' won't come again to trouble you after that, I know.

GAUNT. You are right, lad. There must be no broken

bones, and no bloodshed, being a priest. The horsepond
is the thing. And if you are discharged for it, why,
shoulder your pack, and show the place your heels. I am
off to the " Red Lion."

RYDER. (*Coming forward*) Oh, master, don't go there.
I am sure that is no place for you.

GAUNT. Why not? At the "Red Lion" there is
laughing, daffing, and merrymaking; here there is nought
but praying, and fasting, and quarrelling. That for
Ernshaw Castle; cold, gloomy, and priest-ridden. Give me
the sanded floor and the chimney-corner of the "Red
Lion," with a big beech log a blazing, and lighting up the
teeth and eyes of a dozen jolly fellows that can all sing a
good song, or tell a merry tale. Besides, this is my wife's
house; the "Red Lion" is my house, or any man's that
can pay his shot; so I'll take my heavy heart—to the
"Red Lion."   (*Exit.*)

RYDER. (*Sighs, then turns to* TOM.) Thomas Leicester,
don't you meddle with Father Leonard. Religion is religion;
and if you lay a finger on him you'll never thrive.

TOM. Can't help that. Shouldn't insult Squire. You
see I've passed my word.

RYDER. Thomas, to tell the truth, it does not suit *me* to
have that priest driven away from this house.

TOM. Oh, that is it, is it? *You* have taken a fancy to
his face now. All the better. I did not much like the
job; but now I'll do't with a good heart. Your servant,
mistress.   (*Exit.*)

RYDER. Talk of women's jealousy!

(*Re-enter* MRS. GAUNT *and* FATHER FRANCIS.)

KATE. Oh, Ryder, be good enough to find your master:
tell him Father Francis is just going away.

RYDER. I will bring him to you, madam.   (*Exit.*)

FRAN. Before he comes, I must say a word or two to
confirm you in your decision. (*Very gravely.*) I called at
Leonard's cottage as I came, and there I found a Madonna,
painted by himself; the features of that Madonna were
yours, madam.

KATE. (*Gratified.*) You surprise me. But is there any harm in that? Do not all who would portray a saint, take some woman's face to aid their fancy?

FRAN. That is all very well in Italy, but not here. You are the wife of a Protestant gentleman, and his name is Gaunt; and the foible that runs in his very blood is jealousy. What indiscretion!

KATE. Excuse me; I never sat to Father Leonard. Me sit for the Queen of Heaven! (*She crosses herself.*) You overrate my presumption.

(*Re-enter* RYDER.)

FRAN. In that case, see how full of you that young priest's imagination must be. (KATE *starts, and looks down.*) For it is an exact portrait of you. Humph!

RYDER. Madam, I have found our master. He is at the "Red Lion." He said he would come presently. (KATE *shakes her head.*) If you please, madam, I much desire to speak to you privately, before he comes.

(KATE *looks at her with some little surprise.*) -

KATE. (*Coldly.*) Well; you can wait.

(RYDER *retires up.* KATE *turns and observes her.*)
Be good enough to fetch me a seat.   (*Exit* RYDER.)
The "Red Lion."

FRAN. He will cease to go there when you make his home delightful to him, as it used to be.

KATE. I will.

FRAN. And the girl Jane shall stay?

KATE. With all my heart.

FRAN. And Leonard go to a sphere more fitted to his great abilities?

KATE. I should be his enemy to keep him here. His enemy, and my dear husband's, whose happiness is everything in the world to me.

(*Re-enter* RYDER *with seat.*)

FRAN. I will see Leonard at once, and send him here, to bid you farewell.   (*Exit* FRANCIS.)

RYDER. (Send him *here* ! !)

(*Exit* FRANCIS. KATE *watches him out.* RYDER *places the seat for* KATE, *and stands at her side, a little behind her, watching the effect of her words.*)

KATE. (*Seating herself coldly.*) Well, what is to do? Be brief; for I am in no humour to be worried with my servants' squabbles.

RYDER. Nay, madam; 'tis no such trifle. 'Tis about Father Leonard. Sure you would not like him to be drawn through the horse-pond?

KATE. (*Turning rapidly, and facing her.*) What are you saying? Which of my people would dare to lay hands on a priest in my house.

RYDER. I don't deceive you. They are on the watch for him now; and 'tis a burning shame. A more heavenly face than Father Leonard's I never did see. And for it to be dragged through a filthy horse-pond!

KATE. (*Starting up.*) The villains! the fiends!—Go and desire your master to come to me on the instant.

RYDER. Alack, Dame! that is not the way to do. You may be sure the servants would not dare, if master had not shown them his mind.

KATE. Not one—word—from my servant, against my husband, in my hearing.

RYDER. (*Servilely.*) Heaven forbid, madam! (Proud devil!)

KATE. (*Walking in agitation.*) My Griffith is a lion. This comes from the heart of cowardly curs. Oh, that I were a man! (*Drops her glove—which* RYDER *picks up and secretes.—Pause*) Good heavens! he is coming here almost immediately—by my invitation. I have laid a trap for him. What is to be done, woman? for you are cooler than I am.

RYDER. Why not send him a line, and bid him stay away?

KATE. You are right. But, nay, I promised Father Francis to receive Leonard to-day, and bid him farewell; and indeed I must furnish him with money to go, poor soul.

RYDER. At least, madam, bid him come no farther than
the Grove. The villains won't look for him there.

KATE. But whom can I send? My own servants are
traitors to me, I find.

RYDER. I'll go myself, madam.

KATE. You shall. Run through the wood; 'tis the
shortest way. Fly!   (*Exit* RYDER *hastily*.)

(KATE *seats herself.— Re-enter* GRIFFITH GAUNT, *not intox-
icated, but somewhat flushed*.)

GAUNT. You sent for me, madam.

KATE (*Feebly*) Father Francis was going away.
But you had company more to your taste, it seems.
However, since you are come, be pleased to accept my
excuses for what I said. I forgot myself, and my duty as
a wife.

GAUNT. (*Doggedly*.) I have no quarrel with you, my
dear. You but do what you are bidden, and say what you
are bidden. I take the wound from you as best I may: the
meddling knave that set you on, 'tis him I'll be revenged on.

KATE. You deceive yourself; that holy man would be
the first to rebuke me for rebelling against my husband.
However, he will offend you no more: he is to leave these
parts. You see you were the master, after all. There was
no need of violence. (GAUNT *hangs his head*.) And Jane
keeps her place in your kitchen.

GAUNT. All the better. Come, Kate, I was in fault as
much as you. Let us kiss and be friends.

KATE. Excuse me: you have worked upon my fears,
not my love. Such a victory, over a woman and a poor
defenceless priest—you must be pleased to enjoy it alone.
                              (*Exit sadly*.)

GAUNT. (*Sits down sadly, and sighs*.) Victory indeed!
My heart feels like lead in my bosom. For eight years we
were the happiest couple in Cumberland. That mischief-
making villain has been here but three months; and what
a change!

(*Re-enter* RYDER.)

RYDER (*Soothingly*.)   What is the matter, dear master?

(*He takes no notice of her.*)

Oh, I see : you are down-hearted, because mistress is in the sulks at having to part with her handsome young priest.

GAUNT.   What is that you say?

RYDER.   Oh, never heed what I said.   I am a foolish woman.   I can't bear to see my dear master so abused.

GAUNT.   What d'ye mean, woman?   Speak out, can't ye.

RYDER.   But I am afraid you will hate me.   Dear master, don't you look into women too narrowly; 'tis best to be blind at times.

GAUNT.   Girl, you torture me.   Do you mean to say that priest is my wife's—lover?

RYDER.   Nay, sir, that is more than I know.   But, what I say is, if a cross word from her makes you unhappy, you mustn't drive Leonard from her, or put any affront on him whatever.   And, if you want to see her all smiles again, and loving you better than ever, why you have only to admit that Leonard to the house, and not watch them too closely.   There—there—don't look so.   After all, there's nothing certain.   And perhaps I am too severe when I see you ill-treated   I am sure no woman *could* be cold to you, unless she was bewitched out of her senses by some other man.

GAUNT.   I am a miserable man.

RYDER.   But I won't let you be miserable.   What do we know against her, after all?   She is a gentlewoman, and well brought up; she is not likely to throw herself away.   I'll tell you what to do.   Don't you be so simple as to accuse her to her face, or you'll learn nothing.   Watch her quietly; and I'll help you.   Be a man, and know the truth.

GAUNT.   I will.   And (*with effort*) I believe she will come out pure as snow.

RYDER.   I hope so too.

B 2

(*Enter hastily*, JANE BANNISTER.)

JANE. Oh, Mrs. Ryder, you are wanted. Our Dame is taken badly, and asking for you.

(*Whips up linen and exits, looking back at* GAUNT.—RYDER *goes out hastily.*)

GAUNT. She didn't send for me. But I'll go to her all the same. We have made her ill amongst us—Poor Kate ! (*Exit.*)

SCENE II.—*An Anteroom to* KATE'S *Boudoir.*—*Chairs. Footstool.*

MUSIC.

KATE. (*Speaking feebly at side.*) No, I am better.

(*Enter* KATE, *leaning on* RYDER.)

KATE. All I want now is a little air. Let me sit here. (*Sits down.*)

RYDER. (*Obsequiously.*) Let me put your feet up, madam. (*Does so.*)

KATE. Thank you. (*Puts her hand on* RYDER'S *head.*) Child, you have done me a service, and my husband too. For, if such a dastardly act had been done in his name, he would have deplored it all his days. Such services can never be quite repaid. But you will find a purse in my drawer : it is yours. And my lavender silk, I have only put it on twice, be pleased to wear that about me ; to remind me of the good office you have done me. (*Leans her head back and closes her eyes.*)

RYDER. (Why do I hate this woman, and love where I have no right to look ? I'll take her presents in my hand, and pray by her bedside. Heaven cure my folly, and end my pain.) (*Exit agitated.*)

(*Enter* GAUNT *eagerly.*)

GAUNT. Why, Kate, my poor girl. What is amiss ? Where's thy pain ?

KATE. (*Laying her hand on her heart.*)   Here, Griffith, here.

GAUNT. (*Kneels by her side, and takes her hand.*)   Lean on me, sweetheart; forget all that passed between us this morning.   I dare say we were both in fault.

KATE. I·know I was.

GAUNT. Not so much as I—not so much as I.   Ah, Kate, for eight happy years you and I had never an angry word.

KATE. And.so it shall be again.   I am going to make a sacrifice; a great sacrifice.   No matter; 'tis for you. Will you grant me a favour in return?

GAUNT. Ay, and with a glad heart.

KATE. You once promised to take me abroad.

(*Re-enter* RYDER, *with dress on her arm, and stands in waiting, eyeing them with visible pain.*)

I long to see foreign countries.   After eight years, we both want a change.   I want to be alone with you, far from this place where angry words have passed between us.   (*She throws her arms round his neck—he embraces her.* RYDER *winces*)

GAUNT: I'll roam Europe with thee, my girl, and seek no other company.   But not to-day: thou art not fit for it. Mercy on me, how cold she is; and but now she was burning hot.

RYDER. (*Peevishly.*)   'Tis your fault, sir—you do agitate her.   Let me lay her on her bed, and a good woollen shawl over her.

GAUNT. Nay, I'll carry her thither myself.   (*Supports* KATE—*coaxes and kisses her.*)   Did we worry her and make her ill, poor lamb?

(*He kisses her, and exit, murmuring over her.*)

RYDER. (*Dashing the dress down.*)   Who can bear such torture?   Talk of *his* jealousy; founded on a shadow— while *I* look on and see the amorous idiots.   And now what good have I done myself?   they are fonder than ever.

(*Leans against the door.*) I hear them purring over one and another, fonder now than ever. Oh, agony! Oh, well can I understand what that evil spirit felt when he looked from his place of torture on that fond couple in their garden of sweets. Like him I burn, and freeze, and ache, and pine, and rage, and sicken. (*Pause.*) It needed but a serpent's tongue to spoil that Paradise! Now let me see what a jealous, love-sick, tortured, maddened woman's tongue can do. (*Whips the gown hastily off the floor, as—*

Re-enter GRIFFITH GAUNT.)

(*in honeyed tones.*) Ah, master! where are you going? You look as pert as a peacock.

GAUNT. Well, girl, if you must know, I am going to mount my horse, and ride off all my foolish fancies.

RYDER. She 'twas that told you to ride.

GAUNT. Yes She advised me to have a good gallop for my health, and then I am to dine with her in her room.

RYDER. That was the bait.

GAUNT. What d'ye mean?

RYDER. Don't you see she wants you away?

GAUNT. You are cruel to tell me so. I was so happy.

RYDER. Alas! I seem cruel! but I am kind. (*Knits her brows.*) Let me think a moment. (*Pause.*) Yes. you shall. Mount your horse directly, and gallop him—to Father Leonard's cottage. He is not at home.

GAUNT. Ah! and what should I go there for?

RYDER. Just to see whose picture hangs over that young priest's mantlepiece.

GAUNT. (*Bewildered.*) Whose picture? (*Pause.*) Can't you tell me?

RYDER. I can; but I will not. Be a man, and use your own eyes; don't believe me, nor any woman. Our words are air. Come back to me here, and I'll show you something *I* found there. Come, lose no time.

(GAUNT *looks bewildered and wretched, utters a groan and rushes out.*)

Music, staccato.

(*Enter, on tip-toe,* Thomas Leicester.)

Tom. Hist! Mrs. Ryder.

Ryder. Well, I'm sure. The gamekeeper here.

Tom. Where the hare is, the dog must follow. You are my game to-day. Come, sweet Mistress Ryder, I am suiting to you ever since I came here, and now I want your answer.

Ryder. You shall have it: I decline.

Tom. Don't ye say that. Pray don't say that. You will make me believe it is true what they say in the kitchen, that you are setting your cap at our master. What good can come of that? Come, sweetheart, take a thought. I'm young and healthy; I've got money from the Squire to set up in a business, such as 'tis. I'll work hard and be sober for thee. Say the word now, do.

Ryder. (*Agitated.*) No, Tom, I cannot. I am thankful for your offer, but you must look another way.

Tom. So be it, then: I'll shoulder my pack, and travel. Change is the heart's best cure.   (*Exit.*)

Ryder. Ay, all the men and women in this house are at cross purposes.

Music, strong.

(*Re-enter* Gaunt, *pale.*)

Gaunt. It is *her* picture. I tore it to atoms. There it lies. (*Flings down the strips of torn canvass, and puts his foot on them.* — *Pause.* — *Piteously.*) Mightn't he have painted it without her consent?

Ryder. Of course he might. I don't build much on that. Did you find nothing else there?

Gaunt. No. Oh! if I could only get proof of her innocence, or proof of her guilt! Anything better than the misery of doubt. It gnaws my heart; it burns my flesh. I can't eat, I can't sit down. I envy the dead that lie at peace. Oh, my heart! my heart!

Ryder. And all for a woman not half so handsome as

yourself, when there are others as well to look at, and
younger, and that adore every hair on your head, and
would follow you round the world for one kind look.

GAUNT. Let no one love *me*. I hate all womankind for
her sake. Oh doubt! doubt!

RYDER. I'll cure you of that! See what *I* found in
the priest's cottage.

(*Shows him the glove she had picked up on the green. He
eyes it with horror.*)

GAUNT. My wife's glove! I gave her a new pair last
week. That is one of them.

RYDER. She must have been a good deal flurried to
leave that in such a place.

GAUNT. Oh agony! agony!—But, say she *has* been
there; after all, he is her confessor.

RYDER. Ay, but when an old man was her confessor,
she always confessed in the chapel.

GAUNT. (*Gasping.*) She did. (*Silence.*) Who lives in
the cottage besides him?

RYDER. Betty Gough.

GAUNT. Ah!

RYDER. But la! the mistress did buy her, body
and soul, long ago. No, sir; you had no friend there;
and you had three enemies—Love, Revenge and Oppor-
tunity.

GAUNT. Oh, God! can this thing be? My wife! the
mother of my child! the girl that married me because I
had lost house and lands: the woman that loved me so
truly till this villain came. Abused! dishonoured!
(*Pause.*) No, I'll not believe it yet. I'll take these
things to her, and watch her face when she sees them.
(*Picks up the pieces.*)

RYDER. (*Uneasily.*) That will never do.

GAUNT. Give me the glove.

RYDER. No; no; you'll spoil all; you'll put her on
her guard.

GAUNT. Give me the glove, I say.

(*Tears it from her.* RYDER *utters a faint scream.* GAUNT
*moves towards door, but suddenly turns and confronts
her, but without moving.*)

You seem very loth she should hear your tale.   You want
me to condemn her unheard.   Now, how do I know you
are not a slanderer, and she your victim?   (*A step towards
her*)   You *hate* her; I can see that; and a lie is nothing to
one of your sort.   (*Another step.*)   I'll know the truth;
I'll bring you and her face to face.

RYDER.   What, me tell a lady to her face—

GAUNT.   The truth.   Why not?   Come.

RYDER.   Not for all the world.   I won't go there.
(*Tries to escape.*)

GAUNT.   Liar and slanderer!   (*Seizes her. She screams.*)
I'll drag you to her, but you shall come.

(*Drags her, screaming and struggling, across the stage: she
gets down to his knees, and at last feigns a swoon.*)

Lie there, then, viper.   I'll bring her out to you, that is
all.   Face her you shall.   (*Exit.*)

(RYDER *raises herself a little the moment of* GAUNT'S *exit.*)

RYDER.   I've played a dangerous game, and lost it.
Well, let him kill me; I don't care what becomes of me
now!

A CHORD.

(*Enter* GAUNT *very pale, and stands at door.*)

GAUNT.   She is not there.

(RYDER *raises herself a little more.*)

I tell you she is not there.   Where is she?

RYDER.   Help me up, dear master, and I'll tell you.
                        (GAUNT *helps her up.*)

GAUNT.   I left her too ill to move.

RYDER. (*Feigning weakness.*)   What, don't you know
that women are sick to one man and well to another?

GAUNT.   Woman, don't rack me so; but if you know
where she is, tell me.

RYDER. Nay, I've got a lesson to mind my own business: however, I'll tell you thus much—find *him*, and you'll find *her*.

GAUNT. Ah! I'll find them both if they are above ground.

(He rushes furiously into adjoining room, and immediately returns with a pistol in his hand.)

RYDER. *(Flying at him with great boldness and energy.)* What would you do? Madman, would you hang for them, and break my heart, the only woman in the world that loves you? Give me the pistol. Nay, I will have it. *(Wrenches it out of his hand, and defies him.)* I won't let you get into trouble for a priest and a wanton, you shall kill me first. Leave me the pistol, and pledge me your sacred word to do them no harm, and then I'll tell you where they are. Refuse me this, and you shall go to your grave and know nothing more than you know now.

GAUNT. No, no; if you are a woman have pity on me; let me come at them. There, I'll use no weapon. I'll tear them to atoms with these hands. Where are they?

RYDER. *(After throwing away the pistol.)* If you are a man, and have any feeling for a poor girl who loves you; if you are a gentleman, and respect your word—no violence.

GAUNT. I promise. *Where are they?*

RYDER. Nay, nay; I fear I shall rue the day I told you. Promise me once more: no bloodshed—upon your soul.

GAUNT. I promise, upon my soul. *Where are they?*

RYDER. God forgive me; they are in the Grove.

(GAUNT rushes out.)

I have let loose a wild beast. I tremble. I had better follow him. *(Exit.)*

SCENE III.—*The Pine Grove. (See description in Novel.) Broad lights and shades thrown across the stage to repre-*

sent the effect of afternoon sun penetrating the tall stems of the trees. The ground is covered with fir seeds.

Music.

(Enter Kate *and* Father Leonard *walking slowly.)*

Kate. It seems so ungrateful to part with you, to whom I owe so much. But I console myself by reflecting that it is for your good. You will go to a sphere more worthy of you.

Leon. I have a better consolation than that. Francis has made me see that it is my duty to retire hence, rather than cause dissension between those whom the church, by the holy sacrament of marriage, hath bound together.

Kate. *(Hesitatingly.)* Now, you must not be offended; but Father Francis desired me to—to—supply you with the means to make the journey in comfort. *(She offers him a purse.)*

Leon. *(Declines by gesture.)* Nay, my daughter, Mr. Gaunt might disapprove.

Chords.

(Enter Gaunt, *at back, pale, bloodshot, and, at sight of them, staggers against a tree.)*

Kate. Ah! you do him injustice; he has but one foible; his unhappy jealousy. I will tell him; and I promise you he will approve what I do.

*(*Leonard *is about to take the purse,* Gaunt *rushes between them, drives them apart, and stands a moment, silent and awful.)*

Gaunt. You vile wretch; so you *buy* your own dishonour and mine. Oh! but for my oath, I'd lay you dead at my feet. So, *this* is the thing you love. *(Seizes him furiously and forces him down.)*

Kate. This is some strange delusion.

Gaunt. I must go, or kill! *(Turns his back to go.)*

Kate. What are you doing? *(*Gaunt *turns his face.)* Where are you going?

GAUNT.   To put the seas between me and this hell !
(*Rushes out, as* RYDER *enters, and supports* KATE, *who is
almost fainting.* LEONARD *kneeling, his hands crossed
on his bosom.*)

END OF ACT I.

ACT II.

Scene I.—*The parlour of " The Pack-horse." A brick or sanded floor. Round table with cloth, and knives and forks on it. Cupboard. Griffith's picture hung on wall. Long, low window, with diamond panes and solid upright frame—one casement open. Outside on the sill are several geraniums, through the green leaves of which the summer sun shines powerfully. A butterfly flutters in at the window and out again. A narrow table with a blanket stretched tight over it, iron-stand, basket of linen, small fire with iron at it.*

Music,—*" The Woodpecker."*

Mercy Vint *discovered ironing a shirt.* Paul Carrick *looks in at the window and watches her.*

Paul. Ay, there she is, working for him, and thinking of him.—Mercy!

Mercy. (*Without turning her head.*) Yes!

Paul. Can I speak to you a minute?

Mercy. Ay, surely. Come in. (*Business with shirt.*)

(*Enter* Paul Carrick.)

Paul. I bring ye sorry news, lass. I was in Kendal yesterday, and there I learned that the bailiffs are coming here. Thy father is deeper in debt than he let us know.

Mercy. Oh, this is heavy tidings. But my master that is to be says he will help father.

Paul. Thy husband! A needy gentleman! Eh, lass, how could you think to give me the go-by, and marry Mr. Leicester; a stranger—a man ye know nought about?

Mercy. Now, Paul, not a word against him; or there's the door. How came I to fancy *Thomas Leicester?* He rode to our door, on his black horse, pale and wretched. O, what a face of misery it was! He flung himself into this very chair, and neither ate nor spoke, all night.

Next day down with fever on the brain: and oh, 'twas
piteous. He kept a-crying on one " Kate," in such a
voice brought tears to mother's eyes and mine too. Then the
doctor said he could not live ; and his very shroud was
a making in this house, poor soul. And then you know
I sent for *you.*

PAUL.   And had ye to send twice?

MERCY.   No, good Paul. You were his doctor, I his
nurse. Well, with me being so much about him, and
seeing the strong man weak as a little child, my heart
yearned towards him. He was main cross at first, but
the stronger he got, the gentler and the more grateful.
Nurse and patient, our hearts did warm together, and soon
he saw my heart, and asked me to be his wife. Ah ! he
is coming at last. I hear his voice in the yard.

(*Runs and puts down shirt, and goes to the cupboard, whence
she brings out things for his dinner. PAUL watches her
a moment—then exit with a deep sigh. She does not ob-
serve his departure. Business. MUSIC, and—*

Enter GRIFFITH GAUNT.)

MERCY.   Come, Thomas, why you must be famished.
There, give me your hat, and sit ye down to meat.

(*She puts the hat away. GAUNT smiles and nods to her—
then sits down and goes to carve. She lays her hand on
his arm.*)

MERCY   (*Gravely.*)   Sweetheart, you are forgetting to
give thanks for 't.

GAUNT.   (*Stands up and mutters a grace.*)   I've most
need to give thanks for *thee*, true friend, and gentle mistress. (*Kisses her.*)   Come, sit, and eat with me.

MERCY.   Nay, I dined an hour agone. But I'll sit
down ; for I do love to sit aside thee and see thee eat. It
does me more good than it does thee I trow.

(*GAUNT eats heartily. She fills his cup.*)

GAUNT.   Put it to thy lips, or I'll none on't.

(*She smiles and puts it to her lips. He drinks.*)

Ye don't ask me what made me so late.

MERCY. Nay, that is a question I never shall ask you, master, or I should have you hurrying home, not to be questioned. Early or late you are always welcome to me, Thomas.

GAUNT. (*She is as wise as she is good.*) Well, my dear, I have been to Kendal about your father's debts.

MERCY. (*Laying her hand upon his shoulder.*) Now, Thomas, you know the rule of this room. No trouble, nor care, nor vexation is ever to come here. When you do set your foot within that door, you leave all worries outside.

GAUNT. I know it, sweet Mercy; and here I have found peace, and an angel of comfort. But, to-day, I must 'e'en break thy good rule for once. You know, I have had many a gibe from your father, and your mother too : and last night he said before all his company (he had taken a drop too much, I daresay), says he, " If our Mercy would wed plain Paul Carrick instead of a gentleman out at elbows, we shouldn't be in this mess ; for Paul would help us."

MERCY. Oh ! (*Throws her arm round GAUNT.*)

GAUNT. Now don't you fret about that ! Only, now you know it, don't blame me neither, for losing my temper at last. Said I, " Old man, that is the last of your taunts. I take your inn, your farm, and your debts." "So be it," said he, " before these witnesses." So, the first thing this morning, I had his name struck off the sign-board, and put up " Thomas Leicester ;" and then I rode to the lawyer, and made myself old Harry Vint's bondsman, and got seven days to pay the debts in, and I'll pay them in five.

MERCY. Alas ! Thomas, what have you done ? Why he owes three hundred pounds, I hear.

GAUNT. And I have got two thousand to pay those three hundred withal.

MERCY. Two thousand pounds !

GAUNT. But now comes the bitter pill. To get my two

thousand pounds I must ride fifty miles—into Cumberland; and, worse than that, I must face two people the very sight of whom will be sure to tear open the wound thy gentle hand has closed, sweet Mercy.

MERCY. Then go not anigh them. Send me. I am a good rider I can tell you.

GAUNT. Child, they would not give it to thee. But to me—they must. Not a word more. I can't see thee turned out of the place where thou did'st save me from death and despair. Come, give me my shirt, and let me go, lass.

MERCY. Nay, let me sew a button on first; or what will they think of Lancashire lasses in Cumberland? _Sews button on._) Tell me, master, was Kate a Cumbrian lass.

GAUNT. (_Starting violently._) Kate? what Kate? who? what do you mean.

MERCY. (_Fixing her eyes on him._) Her you cried on so, when you had the fever.

GAUNT. No matter who she was.

MERCY. Oh, I know she is dead. For if _she_ was alive, you could not care for me. You loved her; yet she must die. Poor Kate!

GAUNT. (_Groaning._) Never mention that name to me again. She was not the true friend to me that you have been.

MERCY. (_Gravely._) Say not so, Thomas: for you loved her well. Her death had all but cost me thine. Ah, well, we cannot all be the first. I am not very jealous, for my part; and I thank God for't; thou art a dear good lover to me, and that is enow. (_Embraces him._)

GAUNT. I'd think it little to die for thee.

(_Takes up shirt and exit._)

MERCY. (_Looking after him._) Poor Thomas! I wish he was not so grateful to me. Makes me fear that 'tis gratitude more than liking. Oh, my foolish heart misgives me at parting.

MUSIC.

(*Re-enter* GAUNT *in jack boots.*)

Oh, Thomas, you have got your new boots on. You are really going from me. Alas! if harm should befal you!

GAUNT. Fear nought, my dear; I am well armed and well mounted. My nag's at the door. Stay me not; for indeed I need all my courage to leave thee.

(*He kisses her, and runs out. She opens the window, then sits sadly down, and rocks herself a little.*)

MERCY. 'Tis our first parting. Pray heaven it may be our last! (*Rises with a brave effort.*) Come, to work; that is my only cure. Idleness is the nurse of grief.

MUSIC, SOFT AND PENSIVE, MINOR KEY.

(*She places a handkerchief on the blanket, takes iron from the fire, and tries its heat on the blanket, then is about to iron, but breaks down and lays her head on the table.*)

CHANGE TO MAJOR.

(TOM LEICESTER *shows himself at the window with his pack on his back. He takes it down and sings a stave in praise of his wares.—Tune, the Poacher's song.*)

MERCY. (*Recommencing her work, and scarcely turning her head.*) Alas! good man, you'll find no market here. I've no heart to lay out my money on vanity, this day.

TOM. The worse my luck, good dame. However, I am main hot and dry, so I'll e'en drink a cup with my namesake.

MERCY. (*Looking half round.*) Thy namesake, good man?

TOM. Ay, my name is Thomas Leicester.

MERCY. Indeed! then thou art welcome for thy very name. Bid them give thee bite and sup, and charge thee nought.

TOM. Thanks, good dame.

MERCY. (*Ironing.*) What is this? "G. G," and wrought with fine silk. Silk? 'Tis a woman's hair. (*Holds it up to the light.*) Auburn hair. Something tells me this is "Kate's" hair. " G. G.," what can that mean ?

(*Enter* Paul Carrick, *followed by* Tom Leicester.)

Paul.   Come on, man.   Mercy, lay out a penny with
thy husband's namesake.   It shan't cost thee none.   Come
let us see your wares.

(Leicester *puts down his pack and takes out some lace and
jewels ; but suddenly lifting his eyes, he sees* Gaunt's
portrait and gives a violent start.)

Tom.   Oh, Lord.
Mercy.   What ? you know my Thomas ?
Tom.   (*Still looking at portrait.*)   Not I.   But I know
him that hangs there, of course.   Tell me (in a whisper),
is he alive ?
Paul.   Alive ! of course he is.   That is your namesake.
Tom.   (*Looking.*)   That is *my* namesake, is it ?   Well,
'tis a curious world.   Thank heaven he is alive, anyway.
This will be news in Cumberland.
Mercy.   Belike you are a kinsman of his ?
Tom.   Anyway, you see we are marked alike.   (*Shows
his mole.*)
Mercy.   Dear heart !   How strange.   But how comes
it he is a gentleman, and thou a pedlar ?
Tom.   Well, because my mother was a gipsy, and his a
gentlewoman.
Mercy.   What brought him into these parts ?
Tom.   Trouble.
Mercy.   What trouble ?
Tom.   Well, I daresay there was a woman at the bottom
of it.
Mercy.   Kate ?
Tom.   Kate ?   We don't make so free with her name in
Cumberland.
Mercy.   Can you tell me what this stands for on his
handkerchief ?   " G. G."   (*Shows him the initials.*)
Tom.   Why the first letters of his name.   I do suppose.

PAUL. (*Looking at them.*) How can " G. G." stand for Thomas Leicester ?

TOM. Did *I* say his name was Thomas Leicester? However, he is alive, and got a bonny buxom—wife, it seems. We shall never see him again in Cumberland.

MERCY. What part of Cumberland does he belong to ?

TOM. Good folks, I came here to sell my wares, not to say my catechism ; but you do question much, and buy none.

MERCY. First go to the kitchen, good man, and dine at my cost.

(*Exit* TOM LEICESTER.)

MERCY. (*Sinks into a chair and rocks herself.*) Deceit ! and from him !

PAUL. Nay, lass ; let us not make a mountain of a mole-hill, neither. Mayhap he has got into some trouble, and so was fain to change his name.

MERCY. There is more in it than that. Paul, are you still my friend ? Why do I ask ? I know you are. Prithee, sit down to meat with that pedlar, and loosen his tongue with good fellowship, and learn more from him.

PAUL. I'll do't—I'll do't : and cleverly. (*Exit.*)

MERCY. Deceit !—Deceit ! — a false name. His real name begins with a G.

(*Re-enter* PAUL CARRICK.)

PAUL. Why, what d'ye think ? The pedlar is gone. Took to his heels. Your mother says he just went through the house and took the road, as if he had stolen the silver spoons.

MERCY. He went north.

PAUL. Well, so they say.

MERCY. He has gone to Cumberland, That man found he had told us too much. This decides me. Paul, will you lend me your sorel mare ?

PAUL. And welcome : she is at the door.

MERCY. Put our woman's saddle on her this moment, if you please.

C

PAUL. Your will is my pleasure.   (*Runs out.*)

MUSIC. *Devotional.* (*Boyce's Hymn, " When overwhelmed with grief.*")

(MERCY *kneels down and prays silently. Then rises and takes out a thick veil and skirt. She puts on the hat, and is about to put on the skirt, when re-enter* PAUL CARRICK.)

.PAUL. Mare is saddled. Shall I go with ye ?
MER. No, Paul; not for the world.
PAUL. Why, where are ye going ?
MER. To Cumberland.   (*Exeunt.*)

SCENE II.—*Ernshaw Grove. A cross has been set up at the side, whose shadow falls upon the stage.*

MUSIC TO OPEN SCENE.

MRS. GAUNT *and her daughter* ROSE *enter slowly, hand in hand. Suddenly* MRS. GAUNT *stops, and, half kneeling, examines the child's face earnestly.*

KATE. Her father's eyes. (*Kisses her.*)
ROSE. Mamma !
KATE. My love.
ROSE. When is papa coming back ?
KATE. (*Softly.*) When Heaven pleases.
ROSE. And then we shall leave off this nasty black.
KATE. Yes.
ROSE. I do love papa. He is so merry.
KATE. Rose; *I* was not always sad. (*Aside.*) How cruel are the young.
ROSE. Don't cry, mamma. I love you too.

(*Enter* RYDER *with a tray.*)

RYDER. Mistress Rose, your dinner is ready.
KATE. Go, love. (*Kisses her.*)   (*Exit* ROSE.)
RYDER. You, yourself, would be the better for some nourishment. Indeed, madam, you pray too much, and eat too little. Father Francis says so. At least put this to your lips.
KATE. Since you have taken the trouble to bring it me, I *must*. (*Puts the wine to her lips.*)

Ryder. (*With emotion.*) Forgive me, madam; but this gloomy place will be your death.

Kate. 'Tis a fit place for devotion; and, therefore, fit for me. See these tall pillars, how calm, how reverend. I tell you 'tis a temple not made with hands.

Ryder. Ay, but I don't mean that.

Kate. You mean that here I was foully insulted. I was; and for months I could not bear the sight of the place. But now see, I have set up a cross at the very spot, and there I kneel, and humble myself, and see my own faults, and excuse the faults of others.

Ryder. A hard religion yours, madam.

Kate. All religions are hard to practise; easy to preach. Leave me to my devotions. (Ryder *moves away.*) But I thank you for your sympathy: thank you sincerely.

Ryder. (*Nearly crying.*) Sorrowful, but brave; proud, but grateful. How I should love this woman—if I were a man.   (*Exit.*)

Kate. (*Kneels and eyes the Cross.*)

Music.

Oh anima Christiana, respice vulnera patientis, sanguinem morientis, pretium Redemptionis nostræ, &c.

(*She sinks forward and applies her lips to the shadow of the cross.*)

Appropriate Music.

(*Enter* Griffith Gaunt: *he leans against a tree at side,* l.h., *back of stage.*).

Gaunt. I thought I could look calmly on that guilty pair. But now I am here, I feel I must not. How to see her alone? A woman! All in black?—Who is dead? —It is my little Rose.—Taken from this wretched world. (*Leans against a tree.—Faintly.*— I'll speak to this woman. (*He comes forward.*)

Kate. (*Lifting her head.*) That step!

Gaunt. Can you tell me, my good dame—(Kate *starts to her feet.*) Oh!

Kate. Ah!

(They gaze at one another.—Long silence.)

GAUNT. *(In a whisper.)* In black !

KATE. For thee. For thee.

(She flings her arms round his neck. He shudders visibly, and gently, but coldly, detaches her arms, and withdraws a step.)

GAUNT. *(Gently, but doggedly.)* The day is gone by for that.—Think you I came here to play the credulous husband ?

KATE. What, come back here, and not sorry for what you have done ? not the least sorry ?

GAUNT. For what *I* have done!—There, you are but a woman; and I didn't come to quarrel with you.

KATE. Thank Heaven for that. Oh, sir; the sight of you; the thought of what you were to me once—till jealousy blinded you!—Lend me your arm, if you are a man; my limbs do fail me.

GAUNT *puts out his arm—she leans on it, and trembles hysterically. (Pause.)*

GAUNT. *(sadly.)* Come, come, you needn't tremble so. I'm cured of my jealousy. 'Tis gone along with my love. I am come hither for my own, my two thousand pounds, and for nothing more.

KATE. Oh ! you are here for money, and not for me ?

GAUNT. For money, and not for you—of course.

KATE. Then money you shall have, and nought of me but my contempt. Come, follow me, and you shall have all the money in the house. *(Going out, she lifts her hand to Heaven.)* Oh, how little I knew this man.   *(Exit.)*

GAUNT. Cursed money; you cost me dear.   *(Exit.)*

SCENE III.—*A Lane near Ernshaw Castle.*

MUSIC.

(Enter MERCY VINT.*)*

MERCY. He is gone into that great house. But I always knew he was a man of worship; and would mate below him if he wedded me. Why did I come here ?

Why did I play the spy upon my husband that is to be? He was always good to *me*. Something tells me I had better have stayed at home, and asked no questions. How lonely and weak I feel: poor Lancashire lass, all alone in Cumberland! (*Weeps.*)

(*Enter on tip-toe* PAUL CARRICK,)

PAUL. Who is all alone?

MERCY. Oh, Paul! Didn't I tell you not to come with me?

PAUL. Ay! and so I rode *behind* you all the way; and if your courage had held out, I wouldn't have troubled you: but when you tied your horse to a gate, and then sat down, and began to greet, says I, "Oh dear! Here's a *man* wanted alongside of these here petticoats," quoth Paul Carrick.

MERCY. Good, kind Paul; indeed, I lack a friend and an adviser. He is gone into that great house. What shall I do?

PAUL. I'll tell ye. You shall go to the village inn, and break your fast, and lie down a bit. I'll make the landlord talk, and learn what house this is, and who owns it. Then I'll run back here, and watch the house all night, and tell ye if I see aught.

MERCY. Thank you, Paul. Bless you. (*Going. Turns at the side.*) A friend in need is a friend indeed.

(*Exit, followed by* CARRICK.)

SCENE IV.—*A Sitting Room in Ernshaw Castle, with an oriel window, through which a portion of the mere is seen.*

(*Enter* KATE *slowly, and with feeble steps—she sinks on a couch and moans faintly. Enter* GAUNT, *following* KATE.)

GAUNT. You are ill, madam.

KATE. No, sir; only a little overcome. Be pleased to call my maid.

GAUNT. Who waits?

(RYDER *runs in, and at sight of* GAUNT *utters a scream.*)

KATE. Ay, child; he has come home. His body, but not his heart. (*Holds out her hand for salts.* RYDER *puts them to her nose.—In a whisper.*) Run for Father Francis. He is out in the garden. (*Exit* RYDER *hastily.*)

GAUNT. (*Doggedly.*) Now, dame, are you better?

KATE. Ay, I thank you.

GAUNT. Then listen to me. · When you and I set up together, I had two thousand pounds. I spent them all on this house. Now the house is yours. You told me so, one day, you know.

KATE. Ah, you can remember my faults.

GAUNT. I remember all, Kate.

KATE. Thank you, at least, for calling me Kate. Well, Griffith, since you abandoned us, I thought, and thought, and thought, of all that might befall you; and I said, "What will he do for money ?" So I reduced my expenses three-fourths at least, and I put by some money for your need.

GAUNT. (*Amazed.*) For my need ?

KATE. For whose else ? I'll go fetch it. But first I have a favour to ask you.

GAUNT. What is that ?

KATE. Justice ! If you value money, I value my good name.

GAUNT. (*With calm sternness.*) Mistress, be advised. Rouse not my sleeping wrath. Let bygones be bygones.

KATE. So be it, sir. I will make no conditions whatever, but fetch you the one thing you came for.   (*Exit.*)

GAUNT. Mercy, my dear, I doubt this will be a dear penny to me. Oh, if I was alone in the world, I'd take her money, and fling it in the mere.

MUSIC—"*Little Bo-Peep.*"

(*A door opens softly, and* ROSE *peeps in.*)

ROSE. It is ! it is ! (*She comes running and dancing, and jumps on his knee, and flings her arms round his neck.*) Papa ! papa ! Oh, my dear, dear, dear, darling papa !

GAUNT. My pretty angel ! my lamb !

ROSE. How your heart beats : don't cry, dear papa. Nobody is dead ; only we thought you were. I'm so glad you're come home alive. Now we can take off this nasty black. I hate it.

GAUNT. What, 'tis for me you wear it, pretty one ?

Rose. Ay, mamma made us. Poor mamma has been
so unhappy. And that reminds me: you are a wicked man,
papa. But I love you all the better. It *is* so dull when
everybody is good, like mamma; and she makes me dread-
fully good too; but now you are come back, there will be
a little, little wickedness again it is to be hoped. Aren't
you glad you are not dead, and are come home instead?
I am.

Gaunt. My young mistress, when did you see Father
Leonard last?

Rose. How can I tell? Why, it was miles ago; when
I was a mere girl. You know he went away when you
did. Did he go along with you?

Gaunt. That is strange! (*They are not so hardened
as I thought.*)

Rose. Ah! Oh, what a comfort. They have got out
of that nasty black.

(*Enter Ryder in colours, and places a money bag on the
table. Enter Mrs. Gaunt.*)

Kate. Is she not grown? Is she not lovely? And
more and more like you every day. Surely you will never
desert her again.

Gaunt. 'Twas not her I deserted, but her mother, and
she had played me false with her accursed priest.

Kate. (*Drawing back with horror.*) This, before my
girl?—Griffith Gaunt, you lie!

Gaunt. Ah!

Kate. Oh, that I were a man! This insult should be
the last. I'd lay you dead at her feet and mine.

Gaunt. But, as you are not a man, and I'm not a
woman, we can't settle it that way. So I give you the last
word, and good day.

Kate. Yes, take your money, and begone. I loathe
the sight of you, and curse the hour I ever knew you.

Rose. (*Weeping*) Oh, mamma, don't scold poor papa!
Oh, papa, don't quarrel with poor mamma! (*Runs from one
to the other.*)

Gaunt. (*Hanging his head.*) No, my lamb, we twain

must not quarrel before thee. We will part in silence, as
becomes two gentlefolks, that once were dear, and have thee
to show for't. Good bye, my little Rose.

(*He kisses her. She runs to her mother, who takes her on
her knee.*)

Madam, I am in sore want of money ; but I find I cannot
pay the price. (*Takes a step towards door.*) I wish you
health, happiness, and oblivion. Adieu. (*As he is going out'*

Enter FATHER FRANCIS, *meeting him.*)

FRAN. A word with me, first.

GAUNT. Welcome, thou one honest priest, welcome !

FRAN. Welcome, my long-lost son. Madam, I desire
some private talk with you and your husband.

(*At a signal from* MRS. GAUNT, RYDER *takes* ROSE *out.*)

My daughter, and you my friend. I am here to do justice
between you, and to show you both your faults. I pray
you sit—one on each side of me. (*They sit.*) Catherine
Gaunt, you began the mischief by encouraging another man
to interfere between your husband and you.

KATE. (*Distressed*) But, sir, he was my director, my
priest, my father.

FRAN. Ay, your spiritual father ; but not your temporal
father. You withdrew from society, and avoided your
husband's friends in your own house. In a word, you
bereaved your husband of his companion and his friend.
The error was Leonard's, but the fault was yours. You
were five years older than Leonard, and a woman of sense
and experience ; he but a boy by comparison. What right
had you to surrender your understanding, in a matter of
this kind, to a poor silly priest, fresh from his seminary,
and as manifestly without a grain of common sense as he
was full of piety ?

GAUNT. Ay, that is how it all began. Would it had
ended there.

FRAN. Yet when she found you were unhappy, she was
uneasy, and sent for me. I said " Leonard must go "—she
assented. I went to Leonard, and he is a saint (GAUNT

starts,) though a silly one; he bowed his head to me, a man infinitely his inferior in spiritual gifts; and obeyed me in all humility. He consented to bid Mrs. Gaunt farewell, and sail for Ireland.

GAUNT.   Did you bid him meet my wife in the Grove?

FRAN.   No, my son. But, remember; you had just given your people an order to drag this poor pious priest through your horsepond. Was that well done? Was that like Griffith Gaunt, the brave, the generous? To keep his word with me, Leonard came as near the house as he *dared.*

GAUNT.   But how came my wife's glove in his house?

KATE.   My glove in Father Leonard's house. Nonsense.

GAUNT.   It was found there, and brought to me.

KATE.   Whoever found it there had dropped it there. You have been imposed on. I never was in Leonard's house in my life. I always confessed to him in the sacristy. Father, I appeal to you.

FRAN.   My son, this is so. I begin to think that some foul slanderer has been poisoning you.

GAUNT.   (Have I been a dupe?) No, no! my own eyes have shown me what she is. She can be sick to one man, but well to another. I left her, unable to walk, by her way of it; I came back, and found her on that priest's arm, springing along like a greyhound.

FRAN.   *(A little severely.)* How do you account for that?

KATE.   I'll tell *you*, Father, because you love me. I do not speak to *you*, sir; for you never loved me.

GAUNT.   I could give thee the lie: but 'tis not worth while. Know, sir, that within twenty-four hours after I caught her with that villain, I lay a dying for her sake; and lost my wits; and, when I came to, they were making my shroud in the very room where I lay. No matter; no matter; I never loved her. (*Sobs.*)

KATE.   Alas! poor soul! would I had died ere I brought thee to that! (*Sobs.*)

FRAN.   *(with tenderness.)* Ay, poor fools, neither of ye loved t'other; that is plain. So now let us have your explanation.

KATE.   I lay on my bed weak enough, I assure you.

o 2

But suddenly I thought to myself—oh if I could but settle
it all against he comes back from his ride. So, I got up,
and crept out, and I saw Leonard at a distance in the
Grove. Good Father, *you* know what women are; excitement lends us strength. With me thinking that our
unhappiness was ended—that in half-an-hour I should fling
my arm round my husband's neck, and tell him I had re-
moved the cause of his misery, and so of mine—I seemed
to have wings; and I did walk with Leonard, and talked
with rapture of the good he was to do in Ireland, and how
he was to be a mitred abbot one day (for he is a great man),
and how we were all to be happy together in heaven. This
was our discourse; and I was just putting the money for
his journey into his hand, and bidding him God-speed,
when he—for whom I fought against my woman's nature,
and took this trying task upon me—broke in upon us, with
the face of a fiend; trampled on the poor good priest, that
deserved veneration and consolation; and raised his hand
to me; and was not man enough to kill me, after all; but
miscalled me—ask him what he called me – see if he dares
to say it again before *you*; and then ran away, like a
coward, from the lady he had defiled with his rude tongue,
and the heart he had broken. *Forgive* him? That I never
will, never; never.

    Fran. Who asked you to *forgive* him? your own heart.
Come, look at him.

    Kate. *(Irresolutely.)* Not I: he is nought to me. *(She
steals a look at him.)*

*(Gaunt has his hand on his brow, and his eyes fixed with
horror and remorse.)*

    Gaunt. Something tells me she has spoken the truth.
But if so—oh God, what have I done?—What shall I do?

    Fran. Why, fall at thy wife's knees and ask her to
forgive thee.

*(Gaunt falls on his knees; Mrs. Gaunt leans her head on
Francis's shoulder, and puts out her hand to Mr. Gaunt:—
at this moment enter Ryder with a tray, and stands transfixed.)*

END OF ACT II.

ACT III.

Scene I.—*A Lane near Ernshaw.   Evening.*

Music.

Paul Carrick *discovered walking slowly across the scene and back again more than once, like a sentinel, then retires cautiously.*

(*Enter* Caroline Ryder. *She knits her brows, and appears to meditate profoundly.*)

Ryder. It seems to me there are two things in this world: Passion and Peace. And the two are opposites. And men and women are such fools, they run after Passion, and run away from Peace. For twelve months I have been at peace. My mistress is a noble creature, and has borne her sorrow like a man. I had learned to admire her; I was getting almost to love her: I thought I was cured. But now, at the very sight of that man, the calm is over, and the storm begins again. They will love one another better than ever. I clenched my teeth, and tried to look on their reconciliation. But I couldn't; I was fain to run out of the house. Here I can breathe: here I can think. What shall I do?

(*Enter* Jane Bannister.)

Jane. Oh, here you are, Mrs. Ryder. I've been hunting for you high and low.

Ryder. Indeed! What for?

Jane. Well, you did me a good turn twelve months ago. So now I thought I'd give you a warning. There's something up about a glove. Father Francis did question me whether our Dame had two gloves that day or only one. "She had the pair," says I; "for I did notice them, being new." Quoth he, "Then how could Mrs. Ryder find one of them at Leonard's lodgings? I shall look

into this," says he. So I thought I would tell you.
Forewarned, forearmed, they say

RYDER. *(Gravely.)* I am much obliged to you.

JANE. No, y'are not, or you'd give me a kiss for't.

RYDER. As many as you like.

JANE. I take you at your word.

(JANE *kisses her violently, and then runs out.* RYDER
quietly wipes her mouth with her handkerchief.)

RYDER. That old priest is very keen. He is on my
track. He will get me turned out of this house with a
bad character. I shall be ruined for ever. What in the
world shall I do?

(Enter TOM LEICESTER.)

TOM. Good evening, mistress.

RYDER. Tom Leicester! How you startled me! Welcome to Ernshaw once more.

TOM. I am in luck. You are the one I came to see,
and you are the first I meet. That bodes well.

RYDER. Bodes well—for what?

TOM. For my suit.

RYDER. (Why not? Here's a way out of it all.) La,
Tom, do you still think of me in that way?

TOM. Why not? especially now. Come, mistress,
every dog has his day: the only man that stood between
you and me, he is out of the play. Squire Gaunt will
never show his face in Cumberland again: he daren't.

RYDER. *(Satirically.)* Indeed! And suppose I were
to tell you he is in Cumberland now?

TOM. Then I'd tell you 'tis a lie. He is too well off
where he is.

RYDER. Humph! How do you know where he is?

TOM. I've seen the place. I've seen the little inn he
keeps. I've seen his picture hanging up in it—and—
come a bit nearer—this is between you and me—I've seen
his wife. (She must have been his wife.)

RYDER. What?

(A Pause.)

Tom. Ah, you may well stare. But I tell you he has taken a little wayside inn in Lancashire, and married a pretty dove-eyed woman (Mercy Vint they call her), and ta'en his leave of Cumberland for ever. He won't come here to be burnt in the hand for a felon; and he a justice of the peace: and so I am come post haste to tell you.

Ryder. *(Clenching her teeth.)* Oh! if this is true, he shall smart for it. *(To Tom.)* Such a tale is not to be believed at a word. I must have more particulars.

Tom. Swear to be secret, and I'll tell you all I know.

Ryder. Then suppose you come and sup with me in my room. Will you?

Tom. Thou know'st I'd rather sup with thee than with the king.

Ryder. Would you? Then follow me. Oh!

(Exit, followed by Tom.)

(Re-enter Paul Carrick.)

Paul. Why, sure I can't be mistaken. That is the pedlar, the true Thomas Leicester.

LIGHTS GRADUALLY LOWERED.

He has walked fifty miles in a day-and-a-half. He is going into the house. Mercy must know this at once.

(Exit hastily.)

Scene II.—*The Sitting Room in Ernshaw Castle, lighted by candles. A wood fire burning. Twilight outside.*

Mrs. Gaunt *seated working and smiling.* Rose *seated on a stool, working in imitation.*

Rose. *(Looking up.)* Mamma, you are prettier than ever to-day. I declare you are prettier than my baby. *(Looks from Mrs. G. to her doll.)*

Kate. *(Bowing.)* Oh, madam, you flatter me too

much. What mortal face could vie with those exquisite
features that call you their parent ?

. Rose. *(Examines the doll and lays it on her lap.)*
Well, mamma, at least you are very nearly as pretty.

Kate. Now you are reasonable.

(Enter Jane.)

Rose. *(Pointing to Jane.)* Now look at that! I'm to
be torn off to bed in the middle of a most interesting conversation.

Kate. Yes; but then if you don't go to bed early, you
will never be as beautiful as your offspring.

Rose. *(Shaking her head solemnly.)* Oh, that would
never do. Good night, dear mamma.

(Exeunt Jane and Rose.)

Kate. How long they stay at the table. I hope he will
not be led into excess. Oh, no; Father Francis would
check him.

(Enter Father Francis, who beckons her.)

Fran. Madam, Mr. Gaunt makes me uneasy. There
is something about him very strange. One moment he is
depressed, the next moment he is boisterous.

Kate. Then pray do not leave us to-night.

Fran. I am not my own master. I am sent for to
Underhill's wife, now at the point of death.

Kate. Then I say no more. Let me put you on your
way. The bridge, they say, is hardly safe.

*(She puts her handkerchief over her head while speaking, and
steps out of the window with Father Francis, just as
Ryder enters rapidly and agitated. N.B.—The window,
being open, reveals a powerful moonlight.)*

Ryder. Ah! Those two together. *(Looks after them.)*
No matter; all the priests in England will not turn me out
of this house now. I'll sit here, and wait for her. *(She
crosses her knees, and doubles herself up, like an old woman,*

looking venomous.—A pause.) I think there is but one passion left under my skin: Revenge. *(A pause.)*

(Gaunt's voice is heard, singing a stave. Ryder listens without moving.)

Ay, sing, ye blind sot, and drink what little brains ye have away. I'll sober ye. I'll teach you to reject my love, and then go and give yourself to a stranger.

(Re-enter Kate.)

Kate. *(Aside.)* Why, what is she muttering about? *(Comes and lays her hand on Ryder.)* What is the matter, my good Ryder?

(Ryder turns her head, and looks full at her.)

Oh, what a look! Good Heavens, what has happened?

Ryder. *(Gravely.)* I have just heard something.

Kate. 'Tis about *him.*

Ryder. I don't know whether to tell you or not. *(Poor woman!)*

Kate. What have I not borne? What cannot I bear? Tell me the truth.

Ryder. He has got—a wife—in Lancashire—and no doubt been deceiving her as he has *us.*

Kate. A wife! Are you mad?

Ryder. No. Her name is Mercy Vint. Thomas Leicester, that is in our kitchen now, saw her, and saw his picture hanging aside hers on the wall. And he has taken the name of Thomas Leicester: that was what made Tom go into the inn, seeing his own name on the sign-board. Nay, Dame, never give way like that, lean on me; so. He is a villain, a false, jealous, double-faced villain.

(Gaunt heard singing outside.)

" For wine inspires us, and fires us—"

(Enter Gaunt singing, and half inebriated, with a bottle and glass in his hand.)

Gaunt. Oh, here you are, Dame: you are all traitors

in this house; you desert the bottle. You slipped off at
the third glass. (*A pause—To* RYDER.) She can't deny
it. And even that jolly old blade, Francis, that can put
three bottles under his girdle and never wink, has run
away from good liquor.

(*The women's eyes are bent on him with stern contempt.*)

What's the consequence? The bottle is indignant, and
runs after you? Here, Mistress Ryder, let's you and I
drink to this happy day.

(RYDER *turns her back on him, and goes up.—A pause.*)

(*Beginning to be uneasy.*) This is a freezing reception.
KATE. Too good for you, you heartless creature!
Thomas Leicester is here, and I know all.
GAUNT. You know nothing. Would you believe that
mischief-making knave? What has he told you?
RYDER. (*Coming down.*) If you please, Dame, there
is a young woman wants to see you: her name is Mercy
Vint.
GAUNT. (*Drops the bottle.*) Then I *am* undone.
KATE. Go back to *her!* Me you can deceive and pil-
lage no more. So this was your jealousy! False and
forsworn yourself, you dared to suspect and insult me.
Ah! and you think I am the woman to endure this? I'll
have your life for it! I'll have your life! Give me a
knife, and I'll drive it into his heart.
GAUNT. (*Humbly.*) Here is a pistol. 'Twill do as well.
(KATE *recoils.*) Nay, I would thank anyone to kill me.
I have wronged two honest women, and I am in despair.
Two I have wronged: yet I never loved but one, and that
was you, Kate.
KATE. I'll soon be rid of you and your—love. The
constables shall come for you in the morning. You have
seen how I can love: you shall learn how I can hate.
You have seen how I can endure: you shall know how I
can revenge.

Gaunt. You are revenged already. (*Sinks into a chair, and covers his face.*)

Kate. Send Thomas Leicester to me on the terrace.
                                        (*Exit Ryder.*)
I cannot breathe the same air with *him*. (*Leans against the window.*)

(*Re-enter Ryder.*)

And don't let me see that villain here when I come back: take him to the bachelor's room if he is mean enough to lie in my house; my house it is, thank God!
                                        (*Exit by the window.*)

Ryder. (*Coming down to Gaunt after watching him.*) Well, sir, this is a sorry business. Don't you think you had better have set up your inn with *me*, than have gone and broken the law?

Gaunt. (*Feebly.*) Much better. Would to Heaven I had. Poor Mercy!

Ryder. What d'ye mean to do now? You know the saying: between two stools—

Gaunt. I shall trouble neither. I can't look my wife in the face; and, far less, Mercy Vint: I am not the hardened villain I seem. I lay at the point of death. She nursed me; she saved my life. I was going away; but I found her crying; the reason was plain. I thought to show her my gratitude, and I thought Kate was dead—to me. But oh, how black it looks now. (*Groans.*) And my shame is to be public. The constables are to come for me to-morrow. I am to be accused. –

Ryder. Come, come, you mustn't believe every word an angry woman says. There, take my advice. Keep out of her way for a few days, and you'll see a change. Come, I'll show you to your room.

(*Exit.* Gaunt *follows her, sighing, and hanging his head dejectedly. Enter on tip-toe,* Jane Bannister.)

Jane. Where is she, I wonder? Oh, out o'doors, be-like, for here's the window open.   (*Steps out.*)

(*Re-enter* RYDER, *who knits her brows and reflects.*)

RYDER.   He cannot look either of them in the face, eh ?

(Re-enter JANE.*)*

JANE.   Oh, here you be.   Mrs. Ryder, do tell me the
news.   What is up now ?   For I hear they have had high
words again.

RYDER.   Higher than ever.   But all on one side.   You
should have heard her miscall him.   Why, if you'll believe
me, she threatened his life.

JANE.   Alas ! poor soul: and him only just come back
to her.

RYDER.   If you pity him, take a basket of wood up to
his room; 'tis the little north room they call the bachelor's;
and make him a good fire; for the room has not been used
these three months.

JANE.   That I will; and say you sent it.   *(Exit.)*

RYDER.   And what a time she is — with that Tóm
Leicester.   *(Goes to window.)*   Where have they got to,
I wonder ?   they are not on the terrace.   Humph ! to-night
has opened my eyes.   This woman, that seems so cold,
her passions are more violent than my own.   She made
me tremble.   As for me, my revenge is cool.   He says he
cannot bear the sight of either of *them*.   My chance is
better than ever.   I'll act accordingly.

MUSIC.

(*Re-enter* JANE.)

JANE.   Oh, Mrs. Ryder ! oh, Mrs. Ryder !   He is gone.
The window is open and master is gone.

RYDER.   Good heavens ! who would have thought of
that ?   Oh, the miserable tongues of women !   Well,
Jane, now I believe we shall never see him again.   Stay,
Dick the groom is your sweetheart; bid him mount and
ride south after him, and tell him the mistress says she
will forgive him if he comes back directly.

JANE.   I'll do't: I'll do't.   *(Runs out.)*

RYDER. Will she never come in ? I'll go after her,
and tell her what she has done. *(Goes towards window.)*

(A FAINT CRY IS HEARD.)

What is that ?

(ANOTHER CRY.)

Cries for help by our mere !
GAUNT'S *voice heard crying*—Help ! murder ! help !

A PISTOL IS FIRED AT A DISTANCE,
and GAUNT'S *voice heard again, crying*—Help ! murder ! help !
RYDER *screams violently, and darts out of the window.
Her screams are heard outside.*

(PAUSE.)

Then a murmur and confused cries are heard—HURRY—
pattering of feet inside and outside. THE ALARM BELL *of
the house is rung. Several forms are seen to rush by the
window; then a torch or two seen waving, and* SCENE
CLOSES.

SCENE III.—*The Lane near Ernshaw Castle.*

MUSIC, HURRY, *continued, piano, during dialogue.*

*Several rustics cross the stage rapidly, one after another,
bearing torches.*

(*Enter* PAUL CARRICK *and* MERCY.)

MERCY. What is the matter, I wonder ?

(*Enter* JANE *and* RYDER, *meeting.*)

RYDER. Is Dick gone to the justice ?
JANE. Oh yes ! long ago ; full gallop. (*Exit* RYDER.)
MERCY. What is the matter, my good woman ?
JANE. The matter, quo' she. Why, there has been
foul play done not far from where you stand. Our master's
voice was heard crying murder by the water-side.

(*A man crosses the stage with the drags.*)

See ! see ! they are going to drag the water for him. Oh !
is it come to this ?   (*Exit, hurriedly.*)

(*Enter* MAJOR RICKARDS *and a Constable.*)

RICK.   Good people, is it true that Mr. Gaunt was heard
to cry for help and a pistol shot fired?
PAUL.   Nay, sir, we know not; we are strangers.
RICK.   Strangers! and out so late! Then you must
go with me.
PAUL.   And willingly, your worship.
MERCY.   Mr. Gaunt!   (*Exeunt.*)

SCENE IV.—*By the side of the mere. The water glitters
with the moonlight, and is reddened in places by torches.
Boats with torches are seen moving at a distance in various
directions.*

*Men discovered on the bank holding out torches; confused
murmurs on the water.* MRS. RYDER *discovered. Enter*
MAJOR RICKARDS *and Constable.*

MUSIC CEASES.

RICK.   Which is Mrs. Ryder?
RYDER.   (*Steps forward.*)   Here am I, sir.

(*Enter* MERCY *and* PAUL CARRICK.)

RICK.   Are you sure it was Mr. Gaunt's voice you heard
call for help?
RYDER.   I'd take my Bible oath of it.
RICK.   Do you suspect anyone?
RYDER.   No, sir.   But Mrs. Gaunt had threatened his
life just before.
RICK.   Take care what you say.   Where is she?
RYDER.   She is not in the house; and she has never
been seen since.
RICK.   Was the quarrel very serious?   What was it
about?
RYDER.   Oh, sir, it is no secret now.   Mr. Gaunt had
committed bigamy.   He had married a publican's daughter
down in Lancashire.

(MERCY *starts violently.*)

My mistress discovered it this day, and vowed to take his life.

(RICKARDS *takes notes.*)

RICK. Where was she seen last?

RYDER. On the terrace in company with Thomas Leicester; and, sir, neither she nor Leicester have been seen since then.

(RICKARDS *takes notes.*)

MERCY. Oh, Paul! Paul! (*Trembles.*)

RYDER. My poor master felt his danger and fled from the house. He fled, but met his death.

RICK. You go too fast. ' Time to say that if we find his body.

MERCY. (He has fled to *us.* He little knows what I have learned. Miserable man! Oh, woe is me this day. Woe is me.)

(A CRY IS HEARD ON THE MERE.)

RICK. (*In a whisper.*) Hush! They have found something.

(THE CRY BECOMES LOUDER. MUSIC. *Torches are held out. A boat comes ashore. A group is instantly formed round it, from which, however, men speedily retire horror-stricken.* RICKARDS *and* PAUL CARRICK *go up.* PAUL *comes away, and stops* MERCY, *who is tottering towards the spot.*)

PAUL. No, no. It is not a sight for any woman to look on. (*In a whisper.*) The fish have torn all the flesh off the poor creature's bones. Oh, horrible! horrible!

MERCY. (*Clutching at him.*) Is it he?

PAUL. How can I tell? There is not a feature left, nor a limb to swear by.

(*A cry is heard.*) "Look here! The mole! the Gaunt mole!"

RICK. Ay, the mole: There is no mistaking that. This is all that is left of Griffith Gaunt.

(*Silence.*—MERCY *looks at her handkerchief with dilating eyes.*)

Good people, he was the best neighbour, the merriest companion, the bravest adversary, the staunchest friend. (*Puts his handkerchief to his eyes.*)

             Sorrowful murmurs.)

Silence now. Here she comes. I'll question her on the spot.

(*The people part, and discover a form hidden by a cloak, all but one hobnailed shoe, which protrudes at the same time.*)

      Enter KATE GAUNT, *and takes a position*, R.C.

KATE. (*In a whisper.*) What is the matter?

RICK. Madam, where is Thomas Leicester?

KATE. I know not. He left me hours ago.

RICK. (*To Constable.*) I'll sign a warrant for his arrest. (*To* MRS. GAUNT.) And where have you been since?

KATE. In the Grove, praying.

             (*The people groan.*)

KATE. Have you no sins, good people, or no faith, that you jeer at prayer?

RICK. (*Hypocrite.*) Catherine Gaunt—

MERCY. (Kate!)

RICK. It is my painful duty to commit you for trial.

KATE. Charged with what offence?

RICK. With the murder of your husband, Griffith Gaunt.

(KATE'S *business is as follows, in three clear movements:—At the word "trial," she turns her head haughtily, without moving her body. At "Griffith Gaunt," she draws back and lifts her hands with horror and dismay. Then crosses her hands over her bosom, and lifts her eyes to Heaven.* MERCY VINT *darts forward*, L.C., *and with clenched hands, scans her face eagerly.*)

END OF ACT III.

ACT IV.

SCENE I.—*A Room in the Prison connected with the Assize Court.*

MUSIC PLAINTIVE.

(And then enter JANE BANNISTER, *meeting a* JAILOR.*)*

JANE. Oh, sir, how does it go with the poor lady?

JAILOR. *(Shakes his head.)* Badly. She had a chance till the last witness was sworn. But this Caroline Ryder has hung her : so they all say.

JANE. Oh! who would have believed it of Mrs. Ryder?

JAILOR. And then her being a Papist is against her with a Cumbrian jury. Why, there's a talk of the Pretender making a landing on this coast.

JANE. Alas! poor Dame, is that her fault? They told me I should see her here.

JAILOR. So you will, and shortly. The last witness for the Crown is up, and then the judges will go to dinner, and the prisoner will get an hour to breathe.

JANE. How can they have the heart to eat such a time?

JAILOR. Why not, young woman? *Their* consciences are clear.

(Enter another JAILOR, *who makes a sign, and retires.)*

There, the court is rising. *(He goes out and fetches a chair.)*

MUSIC.

(Enter MRS. GAUNT, *very pale, leaning on the other Jailor's arm. They seat her in the chair, and exeunt. She holds up her cross, and gazes at it.)*

JANE. Oh, madam. Be of good heart.

KATE. Oh, ungoverned temper! ungoverned tongue! Ye have brought my Griffith to death, and me to shame.

*(*JAILOR *re-enters, and beckons* JANE, *who goes out.)*

The gallows! and thousands looking on and hooting me,

and crying "Murderess and Papist," as they did when I
was brought here. Oh that I could die before the trial
begins again.

(Re-enter JANE.)

JANE. *(With meaning.)* If you please, Dame, there is
a young woman to speak with you.

KATE. I can see no one.

(JANE goes out, but returns almost immediately.)

JANE. Dame, if I were you I'd let her come in. 'Tis
the honestest face; and tears in her soft eyes, at you
denying her. "Oh, dear! dear!" said she. "Tell her I
have come fifty miles to serve her."

KATE. Let me know her name.

(Exit JANE.)

A woman come fifty miles to serve poor Kate Gaunt? Ah;
I am not so friendless as I thought.

(Re-enter JANE.)

JANE. Madam—if you please—her name it is Mercy
Vint.

KATE. Mercy Vint!—How dare she? And how dare
you?

JANE. Oh, Dame! your proud stomach it will be your
ruin. Why should you fear her, if she doesn't fear you?

KATE. I fear her not. Only my flesh creeps at her
name. But you are right. Dare she come all this way to
see me; and shall I shrink from her? Tell Mistress
Mercy Vint, Mistress Gaunt will receive her.

(Exit JANE.)

(A long silence).

*(Re-enter JANE, who draws back, and ushers in MERCY VINT
in a hood and travelling cloak. KATE and MERCY look
one another all over in a minute. KATE curtsies stiffly,
MERCY curtsies; but never takes her eyes off KATE. KATE
dismisses JANE by an expressive gesture.   Exit JANE.)*

KATE. May I enquire, madam, to what I owe this visit?

MERCY. Why I have come? To serve *you*, madam.

KATE. *(Coldly.)* Indeed?

MERCY. Alas! 'Tis hard to be received so, and me come all the way from Lancashire, with a heart like lead, to do my duty, God willing.

KATE. Excuse me if I seem discourteous; but you and I ought not to be in one room a moment. You do not see this, apparently. But at least I have a right to insist that such an interview shall be very brief, and to the purpose. Oblige me, then, by telling me in plain terms why you have come hither.

MERCY. Madam, to be your witness at the trial.

KATE. *You* to be *my* witness?

MERCY. Why not? If I can clear you? What, would you rather be condemned for murder, than let me show them you are innocent? Alas, how you must hate me.

KATE. Hate you, child? Of course I hate you. We are both of us flesh and blood, and hate one another. And one of us is honest enough, and *(with some compunction)* uncivil enough, to say so.

MERCY. Speak for yourself, Dame: for I hate you not; and I thank God for it. To hate is to be miserable—I'd liever be hated than to hate.

KATE. Your words are goodly and wise, your face is honest; and your eyes are like a very dove's. But, for all that, madam, you hate me quietly, with all your heart; as I do you. Human nature is human nature.

MERCY. Ay, but grace is grace. I'll not deny that I did hate you for a time, when I first learned the man I loved had a wife, and you were she. But I have worn out my hate. I wrestled in prayer, and prayer did quench my most unreasonable hate. For 'twas the man deceived me; *you* never wronged me, nor I you. But, you are right, madam; 'tis true that nature without grace is black as pitch: the devil he was busy at my ear, and whispered me, "If the fools in Cumberland hang her, what fault o'thine? Thou wilt be his lawful wife." But, by Heaven's grace, I did defy him. And I do defy him. Said I, "Get thee behind me, Satan. I tell thee the hangman shall never have her innocent body, nor thou my soul."

D

KATE. *(Aside.)* Is this an hypocrite? or an angel?

MERCY. So take this paper, madam. *(KATE takes it with some reluctance.)* 'Tis well studied. Build your defence on what I have there set down, and no twelve men in Cumberland will ever agree to hang you.

KATE. Ah!—and you think?—

MERCY. I do think so.

KATE. Bless the tongue that has come fifty miles to tell me that. Bless you eternally, Mercy Vint.

MERCY. Oh, the good that has done me—from her lips!

KATE. Nonsense! What are words, to repay such an act as this? What can I do for you, if I live? *(With great emotion.)* Pray, pray tell me what can I *do* for you.

MERCY. Nothing. *(A pause.)* Yes, there is something. But, before I ask it, 'tis fit you should know my heart. Of course I'll not deny I loved him, loved him dearly. But, madam, when I found how basely he had deceived me, my heart turned against the man, and now 'tis ice to him. Only, when love goes, it leaves the heart aching and yearning; and what I seem to pine for most, in place of what I have lost, is a few kind words and looks from you that have been wronged as well as me; from you that are innocent and unhappy like myself, and that I vow to clear from shame. You are gentle and I am simple; but we are both one flesh and blood, and your lovely wet eyes do prove it this moment. Dame Gaunt—Kate—I never was ten miles from home before, and I am come all this weary way to save you from peril and shame. Oh, give me the one thing that can do me good in this world, a little of *your* love.

(MRS. GAUNT catches her round the neck, and they kiss one another, and rock gently together in a close embrace)

SOLEMN MUSIC.

(Re-enter JAILORS.)

JAILOR. *(In a low voice.)* Madam, the judge is just coming into court. Excuse me—

KATE.   I am ready.   (*Moves away, then suddenly turns.*)
When shall I see you again ?
MERCY.   (*Shakes her head.*)   In this world—never.

(KATE *returns, and throws herself once more into* MERCY'S
arms.   Exeunt KATE *and* JAILOR.)

JAILOR.   You are her witness, my good lass.   I'll take
you in quietly through the grand jury room.

Exeunt.

SCENE II.—*The Assize Court of Carlisle.   The Court as-
sembled —the audience on the other side of a partition with
iron spikes.*   MRS. GAUNT, *dressed in black, in the dock.*

CHORDS.

THE CRIER.   (*Speaking to* MUSIC.)   Oyez.   Oyez.   Oyez.
His Majesty's justices do strictly command all manner of
persons to keep silence, on pain of imprisonment.
THE JUDGE.   Prisoner, this is the last witness for the
Crown.   You can question her, if you think proper.
KATE.   I thank your Lordship.   I *will* put her a ques-
tion or two.

(RYDER *and* KATE *eye one another.*)

KATE.   (*Very civilly.*)   You have sworn that I threatened
my husband on the 15th October.   (RYDER *assents.*)   How
did you understand my threat about the constables ?
RYDER.   Constables !   I never heard you say anything
about them.   I remember you threatened his life more than
once, and bade me fetch a knife.
KATE.   (She has sworn my death.)
RYDER.   And 'twas his life master feared for, when he
fled in the middle of the night like that.   He wasn't the
man to run from constables.
KATE.   Had not my husband, to your knowledge, a
reason for absconding so suddenly : I mean, had he not a
something to fear, quite different from what I am charged
with ?
RYDER.   (*Affecting to be puzzled.*)   You know best,

madam. I would gladly serve you; but I can't see what
you are driving at. (KATE *sighs*.)

KATE. On the 15th October you were in company with
two men, Mr. Gaunt and Thomas Leicester? (RYDER
assents.) Tell the Court what each of those men had upon
his feet.

RYDER. (*Pertly*.) How can I do that? I don't take so
much notice of men's dress as you seem to do.

KATE. (*Impressively*.) Witness, a gentlewoman whose
bread you have eaten, and who is now defending her life,
is a very unfit subject of incivility.

(*Murmurs of applause amongst the Barristers.* RYDER *bites
her lip, but replies obsequiously.*)

RYDER. Madam, I am very sorry my reply offends you.
But, alas! I must tell the truth.

KATE. On the contrary, you have just refused to tell the
truth. Well, did my husband come to Ernshaw on foot
or on horseback?

RYDER. He came on horseback.

KATE. And yet you pretend you don't know whether
he had boots on, or hobnailed shoes.

WILTSHIRE. She does not contradict you, madam; she
only says she did not notice these minute particulars.

KATE. Then she forswears herself. The particulars of
dress never escape a woman's eye Show this slippery
witness the shoes that were found on the dead body.

RYDER. Slippery witness! If you please, my lord, am
I to be mis-called—by a murderess?

(*KATE utters a faint cry, puts her hand to her heart, and
leans against the bar.*)

KATE. My Lord, may I sit down a moment?

JUDGE. By all means, madam. And *you* must not run
before the Court. How do we know what evidence she will
produce? At present we have only heard one side.

KATE. (*Rising.*) My Lord, I welcome the insult that
has won me these good words of comfort.

WILTS. (*Aside.*) This is an able woman.

KATE. Since you refuse to recollect that the gentleman wore boots, and the pedlar wore hobnailed shoes, let us go to another matter. Had Thomas Leicester a mole on his temple?

RYDER. Not that I know of.

KATE. Why, he was your lover. You *must* know whether he had a mole or not.

RYDER. You are right, madam; I think I should have noticed it, if he had.

KATE. Swear one way or the other. Had your sweet-heart, Tom Leicester, a mole on his left temple, or had he not?

RYDER. Madam, he wore his hair low: and, if he had a mole, I never saw it. I hope you won't be offended, but a virtuous woman can have an admirer, yet not know so much about him as you seem to think she ought.

(Pause.)

KATE. Oh, you are a virtuous woman, are you? You *will* swear to that?

RYDER. Ay, madam; as virtuous as yourself.

KATE. (*Carelessly.*) Married or single?

RYDER. Single, and like to be.

KATE. Yes, if I remember right, I made a point of that before I engaged you; and here is the answer in your handwriting. (*Shows her letter.*) Is not that your handwriting?

RYDER. (*After inspecting it.*) It is.

KATE. You came highly recommended by your last mistress, a certain Mrs. Hamilton. Here is her letter, describing you as a model.

RYDER. I have given satisfaction to all my mistresses, Mrs. Hamilton among the rest. My character does not rest on her word only, I hope.

KATE. Excuse me; I engaged you on her word alone. Now, who is this Mrs. Hamilton?

RYDER. A worshipful lady I served for eight months before I came to you. She went abroad, or I should be with her now.

D 2

KATE. Now cast your eye over this paper. *(Paper is handed to* RYDER.) My Lord, it is a copy of a marriage certificate between Thomas Edwards and Caroline Plunkett. Who is this Caroline Plunkett?

(RYDER *is agitated, and makes no reply.*)

I ask you who is this Caroline Plunkett?

RYDER. *(Faintly.)* Myself.

KATE. Why, you swore you were single.

RYDER. So I am : as good as single. My husband and me we parted eight years ago, and I have never seen him since.

KATE. Was it quite eight years ago?

RYDER. Nearly, 'twas in May, 1743.

KATE. But you have lived with him since.

RYDER. Never, upon my soul.

KATE. When was your child born?

RYDER. My child! I have none.

KATE. In January, 1747, you left a baby at Biggleswade, with a woman called Church—did you not?

RYDER. *(Panting.)* Of course I did. It was my sister's.

KATE. Do you mean to call God to witness that child was not yours?

RYDER. My Lord, have pity on me; I was betrayed, abandoned. Why am I so tormented? I have not committed murder.

KATE. What, to swear away an innocent life, is not that murder?

JUDGE. Prisoner, we make allowances for your sex, and your great peril. Examine as severely as you will; but you must abstain from comment till you address the jury on your defence.

KATE. *(Bows respectfully.)* Witness, be so good as to examine Mrs. Hamilton's letter, and compare it with your own. The "y's" and the "s's" are peculiar in both, and yet the same. Come, confess; Mrs. Hamilton's letter is a forgery. You wrote it. Be pleased to hand both letters up to my Lord to compare; the disguise is but thin.

RYDER. Forgery there was none; for there is no Mrs.

Hamilton. (*Bursts into tears.*) I had my child to provide
for, and no man to help me! What was I to do? A
servant must live. Oh! oh! oh! oh!

(*She hangs upon the edge of the box, and weeps.* KATE
bestows a glance of lofty contempt on her, and sits down.)

WILTS. (*Rises.*) Were you and the prisoner on good
terms before this unhappy business?

RYDER. On the best of terms. She was always a good
and liberal mistress to me, and I'd give my right hand if I
could clear her.

WILTS. I will not prolong your most unmerited tortures;
you can go down. (RYDER *moves to go down.*)

JUDGE. But you will not leave the Court till the case is
ended. Officer, keep your eye on that witness. Prisoner,
that is the last witness for the Crown: you have done much
to shake her credit. But there is still a terrible weight of
evidence against you. The Court will now hear you on
your evidence.

CRIER. Oyez! oyez! oyez! Keep strict silence, good
people, for the prisoner is about to speak on her defence.

KATE. May it please your Lordship (*curtsies*), and you,
gentlemen of the jury (*curtsies*), I cannot compete in the
arts of eloquence with the learned counsel for the Crown;
and therefore I will not waste your time attempting it. I
will comment on the evidence; but first I propose to call
an honest witness or two: and I think. when you hear
them, you will see *why* that false witness for the Crown
could not be got to answer certain questions. Of which
my Lord, I hope, has taken a note. (JUDGE *nods assent.*)
Swear Mercy Vint.

(MERCY VINT *enters the box.*)

(*The book is given her, and the oath administered in the
usual form.*)

KATE. Where do you live?
MERCY. At the "Pack-horse," near Allerton, in Lancashire.

KATE. Do you know Mr. Griffith Gaunt?

MERCY. Madam, I do.

KATE. Was he at your place in October last?

MERCY. Yes, madam, on the 14th of October. On that day he left for Cumberland.

KATE. On foot, or on horseback?

MERCY. On horseback,

KATE. With boots on, or shoes?

MERCY. He had a pair of new boots on.

KATE. Do you know a pedlar called Thomas Leicester?

MERCY. Yes, madam, he was at our house that same day.

KATE. Do you know whether he had a mole on his brow?

WILTS. (*Popping up*) Madam, you must not lead the witness.

KATE. Let the question be put in any form you like.

MERCY. My Lord, the truth is, that the pedlar did put back his hair, and show Paul Carrick and me a black mole that was on his temple.

JUDGE. What made him do that?

MERCY. 'Twas to prove himself a-kin to Mr. Gaunt, whose picture he saw hanging on the wall.

KATE. How was this Thomas Leicester shod?

MERCY. He had hobnailed shoes on.

KATE. Where were you when the body was found in Ernshaw Mere?

MERCY. Madam, I was by the water-side. Paul Carrick and I, with scores of folk besides

KATE. Did you see the body brought ashore?

MERCY. I did. And I examined the remains that very night.

KATE. You knew Mr. Gaunt well. Did you recognize those remains for his?

MERCY. Madam, I did not. There was little to go by but the mole, and that methought was a trifle larger than Mr. Gaunt's. And then it had hobnailed shoes on, poorthing.

KATE. Show her the hobnailed shoes. (MERCY *examines them.*) Are those the same shoes the pedlar wore?

MERCY. Nay, madam, I'll not swear that. They are the very same sort of shoes; that I *will* swear.

KATE. Have you ever seen Thomas Leicester since?
(MERCY *shakes her head*.) Nor heard any news of him in
life?

MERCY. None whatever.

KATE. Nor of Mr. Gaunt?

MERCY. Nor of Mr. Gaunt neither.

(*A slight buzz.*)

But something was done at the "Pack-horse" that looks
like the living hand of Mr Gaunt.

WILTS. Oh, this will not do. You must not argue the
case. Confine yourself to facts.

MERCY. I will try, sir. (*Turning to the Judge.*) You
shall understand that on the 14th of October Mr. Gaunt
became bondsman for the debts of my father, Harry Vint,
and undertook to pay them in seven days. Indeed, 'twas
to get the money he went into Cumberland. Well, on the
20th of October, in the dead of night, something heavy was
flung through my father's bedroom window. He struck a
light, and found 'twas a bag of money—four hundred and
fifty guineas. My father read this as I do, and paid his
debts with his bondsman's moneys.

(*Murmurs.*)

(KATE *sits down*. WILTSHIRE *rises*.)

WILTS. What made you notice that pedlar had hobnailed shoes on?

MERCY. I heard them clatter on my floor.

WILTS. That was a pretty story about the bag. Of
course you have brought the bag with you.

MERCY. Here it is.

WILTS. Let me see it. (*It is handed to him.*) Why,
these are not the Gaunt arms embroidered here.

KATE. They are the Peyton arms.

WILTS. So I suspected. Now, witness, the money
you have received came from the prisoner, not from poor
Mr. Gaunt?

MERCY. I can't think that, sir.

WILTS. Don't tell me. The thing speaks for itself.

This bag is *hers*, and the contents were the price of your evidence. When and where were you last in the prisoner's company ?

MERCY. In the gaol, an hour ago.

WILTS. I thought so. And there you two concerted this ingenious defence.

MERCY. Nay, sir. *She concerted* nought. To be sure I told her what I have told here, and did offer to be her witness.

WILTS. For how much ?

(MRS. GAUNT *half rises, but commands herself*.)

MERCY. Oh, sir ! For no money nor reward, if that is what you mean. Why, 'tis a joy beyond money to clear an innocent body, and save her life ; and that satisfaction is mine this day.

WILTS. These are very fine sentiments for a person in your condition. Confess that Mrs. Gaunt primed you with all that.

MERCY. Nay, sir, I left home in that mind ; or else I had not come at all. And, sir, if you please, I'll tell you something I have not told her. I was by the water-side when they first accused her. It fell on her like a thunderbolt ; but she showed no guilt. I ran up to her that moment and read her face, as none but a woman can read a woman's face ; but no guilt could I read there.

WILTS. You seem to have been mighty intimate with Mr. Gaunt down in Lancashire. Pray what was the nature of your connection with him ? (MERCY *is silent*.) I must press for a reply, that we may know what value to set on your extraordinary evidence. Come, you were his mistress ?

MERCY. No, sir ; I have nought to reproach myself with in that kind.

WILTS. You had better tell us that you were his wife.

MERCY. (*Casts a piteous look at* KATE.) No, sir ; I do not say that I was his wife.

KATE. Not married ! !

MERCY. No, Madam. Heaven spared him that crime.

But I should have been—if—Alas! what ill have I done?
I am a poor, deceived, unhappy creature.

KATE. Hush! The woman you insult is as pure as
your own mother or mine. Know, my Lord, that my
miserable husband deceived her, and would have married
her under the false name he had taken: and they told me
he had married her. My Lord, this Mercy Vint is more
an angel than a woman. I am her rival after a manner;
yet out of the goodness and greatness of her noble heart,
she came all that way to save me from an unjust death.
And is such a woman to be insulted? I blush for the
hired advocate who cannot see his superior in this incor-
ruptible witness!

WILTS. Madam, the good taste of these remarks I leave
the Court to decide on. But you cannot be allowed to
give evidence in your own defence. However, I will not
torment your witness as you did mine. The good sense of
the jury will revolt against this romance without any further
help from me! (*Sits down.*)

JUDGE. Call the next witness.

MERCY. (*Piteously.*) What, have not I cleared her?

KATE. 'Tis no use my calling other witnesses. If you
don't believe this one you would not believe an angel from
Heaven. What is all this farce of Justice, and calling of
witnesses, who are only believed when they lie. Do you
want my life? Then take it. It is worth nought to me,
for he I lived for has deserted me and abandons me to the
scaffold.

(*Voice of GAUNT at a distance.*)

GAUNT. (*In agony.*) Ye lie, Kate Gaunt, ye lie.

(KATE *and* MERCY *scream.—Great confusion.*)

KATE. His voice! his voice!

(GAUNT *seen struggling through the crowd, and beating the
air widlly with his hands.*)

GAUNT. Let me come! Let me come! I was on
board ship when I heard.

(He springs into the dock beside KATE, and puts his arm round her neck, drawing her a little behind him: she leans half fainting on him, but must on no account embrace him.)

GAUNT. *(Turning defiantly.)*   Now, then, ye fools—what has she done?

BURST OF APPLAUSE ON STAGE.

WILTS.   It is the man.   I know him.   *(Throws his brief into the air.)*
JUDGE.   Your verdict on *the case?*
JURY   Not Guilty.

(Caps are thrown up, &c.   The Barristers waive their handkerchiefs.)

CURTAIN!

(On the Curtain rising again, the action is advanced a step. MERCY VINT is leaving the witness box, with her hand in PAUL CARRICK'S.   GAUNT and KATE embrace.   THE JUDGE points to RYDER, who is on her knees, and the Officer's hand upon her shoulder.)

The End.

34244

www.ingramcontent.com/pod-product-compliance
Lightning Source LLC
Chambersburg PA
CBHW022009050726
47499CB00008BA/2719